Sh
&
Sweet
&
Sour

Rob Paraman
Flat 3
54 Portland Rd.
Hove BN3 5DL
01273 329082
07891803483

Rob Paraman

Short and Sweet and Sour
By Rob Paraman

© 2003 Rob Paraman

ISBN 0-9544299-2-3

Printed by
Nightwriters Press
SofLuc Ltd, Gemini Business Centre
136-140 Old Shoreham Road
Hove, BRIGHTON
BN3 7BD

Contents

Scraps	1
Rabbit Stew	4
Wing Ding	5
The Escalation	7
The Confession	9
Deadline	12
Room 26	17
The Downfall of Punch & Judy	19
Plaster	21
True Colours	23
Against All Odds	25
Word Play	27
Off The Rails	33
Hi Bloody Ho!	36
Of Mouse and Man	38
Bonkers	41
Reality T.V.	43
The Big Picture	44
The Ultimate High	46
The Phantom Of The Soap Opera	48
Mobius Dick	52
Finding The Words	54
Left On The Shelf	56
Real Trouble	58
Rewind	64
A Change of Heart	66
The Ernest Hemingway Trophy	69
New Rage 1	71
New Rage (Part 2)	75
Guinea Pigs	78
Jesus versus Jesus	79
The War To End All Wars	81
Hounded	82
Harold Wolfrey's Last Christmas	83
Seeds	86
Strawberry Wine	87

If Only –	89
Roundabout	91
The Last Assignment	93
The Three Way Split	95
It Never Did Me Any Harm	96
The Very First Day of Peace On Earth	98
Generations	99
Bolt-Ons	101
Very Late	104
Natural Selection	106
The Tide Turns	107
Players	110
The Self Portrait	113
Paper Anniversary	115
Twister	118
Anarchy In The U.S.A.	120
The Invasion	122
Goddesses	123
Speed Dating	124
The Great Escape	125
Bestiality	128
Too Big For My Boots	131
The Electric Hare & The Silicone Bunny	132
Reality T.V.	134

Scraps

Jesus ordered fish and chips and a cup of tea. Maureen kept on wiping down the next table over and over again, trying to overhear what was being said. The Buddha ordered a baked potato with cheese and a large orange juice. I glared at Maureen, insinuating she get back to the kitchen. Krishna ordered baked beans on toast with a camomile tea.

Now, don't think for one minute I'm silly enough to go spouting things I heard and half-heard being said at table five on that Wednesday afternoon. That could get a bloke into all kinds of trouble. But what I will say is that there was a lot of laughter and a peaceful atmosphere manifested that you could feel the minute you walked into the café. Of course when the food was ready, Maureen and I made double sure everything on the plates looked just right before it left the kitchen: nudging a baked bean here; repositioning a chip there. I carried the three plates with Maureen following right behind me with the drinks on a tray. Just as I was placing the last plate on the table, Maureen went and spilt some orange juice onto the baked beans. Normally I would have seen red and bawled her out when we returned to the kitchen. But for some reason, at that moment, I had a complete understanding that accidents happen to everybody and getting angry was nothing but a waste of energy. The only important thing, at that moment, was to soak up the spillage, top up the Buddha's orange juice and offer to replace Krishna's baked beans while profound apologies were expressed. Krishna smiled and gestured that it wouldn't be necessary.

Naturally Barney, our chef, didn't believe us when we told him who was at table five — couldn't blame him really. So he took a peek into the café. "Jesus Christ!" he gasped. "I don't know which one's which, but I can feel the vibes from here, man. It's amazing!" Even after the three had left the café, a serene atmosphere remained. Miraculously, the three of us had not one argument all afternoon which was a first. Somehow, we all had an insight into each other's role in the workplace and indeed in the world at large. By closing time, the whole place sparkled like never before. The three of us had our customary fags by the back door.

Maureen laughed: "Imagine what they'd say if we went to a newspaper!"

Barney shook his head. "We'd all get put in a mental asylum! It's a pity we didn't think about keeping some sort of evidence or souvenirs of their visit."

"Yeah!" I added. "We don't even know which dishes they used. And they paid in coins, so I don't know which ones they handled."

Barney said he was going to stay on for a bit that night because he wanted to sort out the fridge for tomorrow. At first I thought that this was all part of the new "good vibes" thing. It wasn't until I was halfway home that it hit me.

"The tablecloth! It'll be in the laundry bag with the telltale stains on it! So that's why Barney's hanging around, the sly bastard."

I raced back to the café and slipped in the back door. I felt ashamed when I found Barney rearranging stuff in the fridge.

"Barney, we forgot about the tablecloth they used. We can divide it into three and all have our own mementoes!"

Just then Maureen appeared.

"So what's going on here, then? Did you two think I was stupid enough to forget about the tablecloth?"

She snatched up a carving knife and, for a moment, I thought that she was going to carve up the both of us. Instead she headed for the laundry basket, snatched up the stained cloth and slashed it into three pieces. She tossed the two least stained pieces to Barney and me.

"I should have known you two arseholes would conspire behind my back!"

Then she strutted out.

Afterwards, at home, I gazed at my piece of cloth until late in the evening. Then it dawned on me that the stains didn't match up with the seating arrangement. Barney must have nicked the real relic and stained a replica for us to find.

"THAT's what he was doing in the fridge, the arsehole!"

He didn't turn up for work the next day and we never saw him again. I didn't have the heart to tell Maureen about the switch. She kept taking more and more time off work, finding symbols and messages in the stains. I think she lost her marbles in the end. One thing's for sure: if I ever see that Barney again, I'LL MURDER THE BASTARD!

Rabbit Stew

Bernie yells, "Shit, we just hit a rabbit!" Rainbow Daryl says, "We'd better go back and hit it on the head. It could still be alive." Richard says, "Still alive? This ute weighs three fuckin' ton'. That rabbit'll be flat as a pancake." Bernie puts his foot on the accelerator.

Rainbow Daryl pleads, "But how can you be sure, Richard? It might be just injured. Imagine the pain it could be sufferin' right this minute." Bernie slows the car down.

Richard says "You heard the whack, Daryl, the fuckin' thing's dead. Rabbits die every day out there in the bush: they get caught in traps; they get myxomatosis; foxes eat 'em. Getting' hit by a ute is the best way for a rabbit to go." Bernie hits the accelerator again.

Rainbow Daryl yells "That's a sentient being back there, man. It's fuckin' bad karma treatin' fellow creatures like shit. Turn back Bernie, else you'll pay for it in the next life!"

Bernie takes a long breath and pulls the car over. On the way back we hit a sheep.

Wing Ding

Once upon a time in a land not far from here there lived ten left-wing politicians and ten right-wing politicians. All they ever did was argue and disagree with each other, so one day they all decided to get together in an attempt at coming to some sort of understanding.

The meeting started peacefully enough but before long faces started to redden and accusations began to fly. Firearms appeared on both sides of the room and a deafening shoot-out ensued. Tables were upturned and the room filled with blue smoke. Then came an eerie silence. Out from behind a table emerged four right-wing politicians.

"We did it, boys!" yelled Richard triumphantly. "That's the left-wing fraternity completely wiped out."

Then they all linked arms for a singsong. All, that is, except for Alan, who seemed to be unhappy about something.

"What's the matter, Alan? Don't you understand there's no more left-wing idiots to spoil our lives?" asked John.

"Yes, John," said Alan coldly. "But you were never as right-wing as the rest of us, were you?"

"No, Alan, I can't say I was but I am a right-winger all the same, aren't I?"

"Well, John, things just AREN'T the same now, are they?" seethed Alan. "Don't you understand, Johnny Boy, you ARE the NEW LEFT!"

Without warning Bernard pulled out his gun and shot John dead on the spot.

"Nice one, Bernie!" said Alan. "I could see that left-wing look comin' into his eyes!"

But Alan's jaw dropped as Bernard pointed his gun at him. "W-what are you doing, Bernie — have you lost your mind?"

"You were never as extreme as Ben and I, were you, Alan? The trouble is, the centre of balance has moved along under your feet, old boy!"

BANG!

Ben looked at Bernard and Bernard looked back at Ben. Ben knew very well that Bernard was the most extreme right-winger ever to step into the political arena.

"Oh, shit," said Ben, "I'd rather be dead than Red!" and promptly shot himself in the heart.

Bernard looked in disgust at all the left-wing fodder that surrounded him. All of a sudden an evil ghost seemed to have entered his body.

"Oh, my God!" he screamed. "I'm half left!" and with that he shot his own left arm and leg off. He fell to the floor and with his dying breath whispered: "Shit, I'm still half fucking left!"

But the sad tale doesn't finish there, my fellow voters. Bernard then felt himself rising up to the heavens, spiralling uncontrollably. Amongst the clouds, he could see his old buddies. Strangely they were all paired off arm in arm with — of all people — the rotten old left-wingers.

"What are you doing?" he sang out in his angel-like voice.

"Bernard!" sang Alan in reply. "Take a look over your shoulder!"

Bernard looked over his right shoulder to see a beautiful white-feathered wing flapping away.

"Now check your left side!" Bernard was astonished to find nothing but his shoulder blade. "That's why you're spinning around, Bernie; you're lop-sided — you only have a right wing!"

Bernard quickly found an unattached left wing mate to cling to and they soon mastered the art of flapping in unison. And they all flapped happily ever after.

The Escalation

Once upon a time, at two a.m. to be exact, all the toys in Jimmy's playroom assembled on the playroom floor. They all stood to attention in a straight line while the plastic soldier paced back and forward.

"I have called everyone together" he barked, "because this afternoon I heard on the news program that there is a lot of turmoil in the big world outside. I think it is high time we all began to think about our own security here in the playroom. For example: what is stopping other toys from other playrooms just marching straight in here and throwing us all out into the cold?" All the toys looked at each other in astonishment.

"Allow me to draw your attention" he continued, "to the big wooden train in the corner – as you can see, I have made a few modifications to it." Everyone walked over to see. "I have slotted Jimmy's sling shot into the front funnel, so that its two arms with the big elastic band protrude from the top. I shall sit on the engine directly behind the sling shot so that I can operate it. There are seven carriages attached to the engine – one for each toy to sit upon. Teddy Bear will sit backwards on the caboose and power the train along with his legs. I have placed three ping pong ball bombs behind the engine at the ready, in case we need to fire them with the sling shot – so lets all jump on board now so that we can patrol the house!"

Everyone jumped on board and the wooden train rolled out of the playroom and down the passageway.

"Stop the train!" commanded the soldier. Everyone passed the message along; the teddy bear brought the train to a stop.

"Look up there ahead," he whispered. "See? Hiding in the shadows!" The defence force looked in terror at the approaching invaders. "Don't just sit there, Mr Robot, pass me a ping pong bomb!"

TWWAAANG! Off it flew down the hall. But they were instantly met with retaliatory fire. Teddy Bear was hit square on the forehead and collapsed on the carpet. Everyone jumped off the train and lifted him back on board, then reversed the train back into the playroom and slammed the door shut behind them.

"Did you see those savage faces?" gasped Action Man.

"I told you all, didn't I ?!" shouted the breathless soldier, "We are all in imminent danger here. Did you see their weaponry of mass destruction? Look what they've done to poor Teddy! I was hoping it wouldn't come to this, but we're going to have to upgrade our artillery. I've made a stockpile of Jimmy's king size marbles behind the rocking horse – come on – let's load up the train on the double. We haven't got much time!"

Again, the wooden train edged out of the playroom and inched its way back down the hall. The soldier signalled to halt. A king size marble was loaded into the slingshot, then everyone helped to pull the big elastic band back and take aim.

"Fire one!"

There was a big TWANG followed by a deafening smash, as the hall mirror fell to the floor before them.

The Confession

She knew there was something wrong as soon as she stepped in the house: the television was off and Justin was in his bedroom. I was on the couch staring straight ahead. She just stood there in the doorway looking at me, then she noticed her mobile phone sitting all alone in the dead centre of the coffee table.

"Who is M, Rhonda?" I asked, without looking up.

Slowly she came forward and picked up the phone. She read the text message and looked all surprised.

"I don't know who the hell it is, Rick, I really don't!"

"Oh right", says I, keeping my voice as clear and steady as I can, "so M, - who you don't know – sends four fucking messages to a different Rhonda who just happens to have the same phone number as you – do you think I'm fucking stupid or what? One of them even thanks you for a good time out last Saturday while I was banged up. Now, correct me if I'm wrong – but there seems to be a continuous chain of communications going on here – what do you fucking take me for?"

She turns on the waterworks.

"I don't know what's going on – I really don't – someone must be playing a joke on us or something!"

That's when I lost it – I slammed both fists down on the glass coffee table.

"A fucking joke? " I screamed "Ho! Ho! Fucking ho! Someone is banging my Mrs behind my back – oh very fucking funny!"

I jump up and grab a fist full of her hair.

"If I find out who it is – I swear I'll fucking kill em – they're fucking with people's minds here – I don't care if I go back to jail – I'll kill the bastard – just tell me who it is Rhonda – who the fuck is M? – you must be able to trace the number or something?"

She looks all-innocent "I keep trying, Rick, but it always comes up as anonymous!"

"But, surely the police can trace it can't they?"

"I don't know, Rick!"

"Well, you don't sound too fucking keen to me – can they trace it or not?"

She goes to shrug so I slap her to the floor.

"Who the fuck is M? – Tell me Rhonda!"

She's holding one arm up to protect herself. Justin runs in crying and lays over the top of her. I'm hyperventilating, so I sit back on the couch.

"Just give me one fucking name Rhonda – one fucking name – then we can forget this marriage!"

She's holding her face and shaking her head "If I knew who it was, Rick, I'd fucking well tell you. I've asked around work and they're all blaming each other. Noreen and Kelly say it's Sue Griffith – Sue Griffith reckons it's Penny McKindoc, but I don't even know her. Charlotte Snow says Penny is a lesbian and is trying to ruin my marriage."

"Oh fuck" says I "my wife's turning lesbian on me now – am I not good enough for you anymore, Rhonda – is it because I'm out of work and can't raise it anymore?"

"Rick, please!" she starts wailing "I've never even looked at anyone else – you're all that I've ever wanted – I've always loved you."

"Rhonda, just tell me one name – I'll accept it – just confess now and I won't get angry – maybe someone just eyes you up at work – you must know who they are for God's sake – someone you sit with at lunch or share a fag break with?"

She gets up off the floor holding Justin who's hiding his face in her hair "Rick, you have got to believe me – nothing is going on!"

I bury my face in my hands "I don't know what to fucking believe anymore – what am I supposed to think of 'thanks for a great time on Saturday – kiss – kiss – kiss'? What do you fucking take me for? Just confess and I'll move into my mum's spare room with Justin – we can't live a lie anymore. Please don't make me go to your work and track down everyone whose name begins with 'M'. Don't make me do that Rhonda. Save us both all that embarrassment, just confess it to me now, no more silly games, then I can take my son and you can start a new life with whoever 'M' is."

Then she starts really blubbering "You can't take Justin away from me – he belongs here!"

"Well, stop fucking around behind my back!" says I. "I must be the laughing stock of your factory!" Then I pull out the hammer from behind the cushion and crack her one over the skull. "Just fucking confess!" I screamed "Confess! – Confess! – Fucking confess!"

There was a lot of blood – always is – but she made it to work the next day. I let things simmer down for five days before I sent her the next message. She'd never guess 'M' stood for me.

Deadline

The coldness attacked him. There were no neatly folded clothes to greet him this morning. A pain ignited deep in the core of his brain that flickered and grew, as he darted across the room. Whilst pulling open drawers and searching for clothes, he calculated that if he could run to the station in seven minutes he could catch the 7.45, taking him on to his destination for 8.22. It always took him fourteen minutes to march from the station to work, but, if he ran all the way, he could get there for 8.27 — twenty-seven minutes late. The birds singing outside served as a nagging reminder that he was behind time. He was never late. He allowed himself a quick visit to the toilet and a mouthful of icy water from the tap, before grabbing his coat and pushing his cap down over his tousled hair.

His body wasn't ready for running. The pain in his skull reverberated every time his boots slapped the pavement. He thought that he was going to vomit, but the feeling subsided, as he eased the pace for a few seconds. He cursed the ticket man under his breath: Look at how slowly he moves! Has he ever had a single responsibility in his life? His ears pricked to the sound of his approaching train. Drawing on his last reserves of energy, he took the stairs up to the platform by threes, groaning with exhaustion as he reached the top. He fell into a seat and a dizzy emptiness overcame him. His clothing clung to his moist skin, as he gasped for air. He heaved forward, coughed and then dry retched.

His carriage was dotted with strangers, leisurely thumbing through the day's newspapers, but he had no interest in the headlines this morning. Then, he wondered if the people on the earlier train would have noticed his absence and, if so, where would they think he was now? His breathing eventually steadied but the nausea took a stronger hold over him.

The evening before had started quietly enough: just a few drinks planned with his wife and friends to celebrate his promotion. As the gathering had toasted and nibbled on warm cake, fresh from the oven, he had explained to everyone that the new position wouldn't be easy. There would be new responsibilities on his shoulders. Being second in charge, he'd have over fifty workers under him. His predecessor had allowed figures to slip over the last quarter and, only a week ago, through lack of supervision, one worker had to be replaced after sustaining third-degree burns to his hands from not wearing the gloves provided. The night shift was proving to be 23% more efficient with fewer staff — staff who worked together, the different departments synchronised, not squabbling over who should be doing what. Now it was his chance to step in and get the workers motivated again, to inspire commitment and dedication in every individual no matter how menial his duties might be.

Later on in the evening at the table, Stephanie Fischer had asked the couple what they were going to do with the extra income. He'd answered proudly that he'd thought of investing in a car. It was then that his wife Anna added: "After the pram, dear."

There was a stunned silence: everyone turned to him questioningly, mouths agape, then back to Anna again.

"Yes, I'm pregnant!" she declared giddily. There was a triumphant cheer, as he raced round the table and embraced her.

"Well, you could at least have told me first!" he stammered, to an explosion of raucous laughter.

Then came a new round of toasting and congratulating, the new cause instantly doubling the speed at which the beer and wine flowed. Before long, faces began to glow, pronunciations began to slur and laughter rose even higher into the night.

He spoke enthusiastically about the power of positive thinking, having the courage to stand up for what one believed in and taking responsibility. Peter and Bert used to loan him money every month when his rent was due, when he was sweeping floors and pushing trolleys for a living. That was a few years ago. Now he was actually loaning money out to them and cheerfully extending the repayment times whenever it was requested.

As the evening wore on, he theatrically imitated his boss'

voice telling the gathering how he had received the news of his promotion. "You have been chosen over five other men," he began in gruff mock seriousness, "men who are older than yourself, good hard workers who know the equipment and procedures just as well as, if not better than, yourself," he continued, raising his eyebrows. "The factors accounting for your being chosen over the others are that: you are trustworthy; you haven't missed a working day since your appointment here two-and-a-half years ago; you're never late; and you don't drink too much." Everyone laughed as he held up his glass and took a gulp and then added: "What I need is a man beside me whom I can rely on 100% and I think I've made the right choice — congratulations!" Then he vigorously shook Peter's hand to demonstrate his boss' enthusiasm.

Now, here he was, sitting helplessly on the late train. A gap appeared between the left-hand side of the minute hand and the uppermost digit on the watch face. These very men over whom he'd been promoted would now be gleefully waiting for him to arrive and allocate workers their day's duties. Anna had given him the watch for his birthday; it now seemed to be betraying him, the cruel hands drawing away from the important numbers. He imagined an ant crawling about beneath the glass, then wondered if the hands would scissor it. He didn't dare to wind his watch this morning, fearing that it would encourage the hands to go even faster.

He wanted to yell at his wife for neglecting to set the alarm for this, the most important day of his career. Then he recalled that a few nights ago Anna had remarked:

"I may as well not bother setting the clock if you're always going to check it after me."

As the journey continued, new perspiration broke out over his forehead and scalp and his face began to feel cold and wax-like. He pressed his hands alternately into the seat either side of his body to counteract the unpleasant manoeuvring. He tilted his head back and concentrated on keeping a steady breath, then closed his eyes. He felt as though he was floating. There was no escaping it this time. He lurched forward away from the aisle. It hurled forth in a gush, warm and foul, splashing on the floor. Tears welled in his eyes as he shivered and convulsed. Its colour startled him, till he realised it was the cake his wife had baked the night before. He heard the other two passengers in his section making their way up the aisle away from the revolting sight and odour. A string of saliva joined his mouth to the floor. He felt embarrassed and ashamed but relieved to know that he'd never have to face those passengers again. The putrid taste remained and the acid burned his throat.

At last the nausea had lifted and he imagined what lay ahead of him at work. Frank would surely ask him in front of everyone if he'd brought the afternoon newspaper with him, a stale joke that he always enjoyed asking latecomers himself. Everything would be 27 minutes behind schedule because of himself, and today being Thursday was always the busiest day of the week. What an example to set on his first day in charge! He wanted to punch the seat in front of him. He was never late.

The train lost its momentum and shuffled along the last few hundred paces of track to the station. "Why are they doing this?" he muttered to himself as he wiped his mouth with his handkerchief. "Why can't we just go directly into the station in the usual manner?" Now he wanted to push the seat in front of him to make the train go faster. He imagined the driver to be half-witted and to look somewhat like Frank.

There could be no excuse. The boss would see from his first-storey window that the trains were dead on time. He finger-combed his hair as well as he could, utilising the moisture from his forehead. The low peak of his cap would shield his eyes from the sunlight and the people he had to deal with. He tried polishing his new badges and regulation boots, as if they could compensate in some way for his ineptitude.

He bounded from the carriage before the train had stopped, nearly tumbling over on impact. One of his new responsibilities was to ensure that the security procedures were carried out prior to the arrival of all freight trains, the first delivery due in thirty minutes from now. He stole two mouthfuls of water from the men's bathroom, pushed past the ticket man, ran through the station and up the dirt road. If he was lucky, a military vehicle might come along.

An unbroken ribbon of red smoke trailed into the cloudless sky ahead. His superior must have come all the way down from his office to assign the duties himself; he hoped that he had not entrusted the command to any of the other men, especially Holder. Holder would even turn the oven temperatures up, inviting untold problems later in the shift. As he neared the camp, there was the accustomed smell of burning human flesh.

Room 26

"Good Evening Sir, are you here for the meditation Class?"

The young man in the sharp suit gave the old Indian woman a blank look. "Meditation class? There must be some mistake, Madam. You do know that you are now in Room 26, don't you?"

"Yes Sir, Room 26, and my students should be arriving here in approximately ten minutes."

The young man put his brief case on the desk. "But that can't be right. I'm teaching the Assertive Training Class here in ten minutes from now!"

"I think you're mistaken Sir because it says here in the 2004 Evening Class Programme that the Meditation Group will meet right here every Tuesday evening at 7.30 p.m."

The Assertive Training teacher rubbed the back of his neck. "But Madam, if you care to take a look on the next page you will see that my group has also been listed as meeting here every Tuesday at 7.30 p.m. The Administration people who have these things printed up are always making errors. I'd get on the phone to them first thing in the morning if I were you, because now your group has nowhere to meet tonight: all the other rooms are occupied."

"But Sir, the Meditation Group has been meeting here for the past twelve semesters!"

The young man shrugged apologetically. "That's what I mean about the Admin in this place: they're hopeless. What they've obviously done is transferred the Assertive Training Course from room 9 to here without allocating you poor soles a new venue! And please, Madam, stop moving those chairs away. My students will need those to sit on!"

A thickset man with tattoos on his neck arrived at Room 26. "Are you both here for the Anger Management Course?" he asked.

"No, we're not here for the Anger Management Course!" spat the Assertiveness Training teacher. "I was just saying to our Meditation Guru here that the Admin Office has muddled up the programme and triple booked Room 26. Now, if you'll both kindly vacate my classroom. I'd suggest you both call the Admin Office first thing tomorrow morning. You'll find the number at the back of the programme. Hopefully, they've printed THAT right!"

The meditation teacher moved towards the door, but the Anger Management teacher stayed put.

"I think you'd better just calm down for a minute, Pal. I can see you're carrying a lifetime of pent up anger around with you. Now, if you'll just close your eyes for 30 seconds and relax your whole body – I'll do the same – then we'll mentally take one step back from the problem, open our eyes, take one step forward and give each other a big hug."

"Fuck off, homo! This is my classroom!"

"Oh, is it now, Mister Administrator. Well, my students might not take too kindly to some smart arse in a collar and tie telling them to get off their own turf. Some of my students have recently returned from their holidays at Her Majesty's Pleasure and can get mighty sensitive about such issues!"

"Oh, is that right, Mister Bully Boy? Well, I can tell you RIGHT NOW that nobody, and I mean FUCKING NOBODY, FUCKS with the Assertiveness Training Group! So if you and your students want to settle this in the car park with me and my students, be my guest!"

An all in fight ensued in the College Car Park. Both parties were taken away kicking and screaming in separate Police vans. A few minutes later the meditation group arrived at Room 26.

The Downfall of Punch & Judy

The curtain falls but there is still frantic activity going on behind it. "Judy, can't you ... OOF! ... See, the show is over?"

Judy growls, "this is what you get for head-butting me!"

"But, Judy, the reason ... OOF! ... I head-butted you was because you tried to gouge my eyes out"

"Punch, the reason I tried to gouge your eyes out was because you tried to rip my nose off my face."

"But, Judy, we'll really have to stop this, otherwise we'll end up ... OOF! ... killing each other."

Judy freezes in mid-swing. You mean, be friendly to each other?"

"Yes!"

"But Punch and Judy can't be friends. We're MAD to hit each other, I know, but it's what the audience expects. If we didn't hit each other they'd want their money back and Punch and Judy would be no more."

"Judy, we can at least be friends between shows, can't we?"

"But Punch, every time you hit me, I just have to hit you harder and I just have to get the last hit ... OOF! ... in. What was that for?"

"I owed you a big one for those last three hits."

"Punch, do you think there's some kind of evil force that's driving us to destroy each other?"

"Yeah, come to think of it ...OOF! ... it does seem that way. I bet the Devil gets his kicks out of our ...OOF! ... suffering."

An enormous grinning head appears between the two puppets causing them to shake likes leaves in a hurricane.

"Oh my God! It's the Devil himself."

"Ha, Ha, Ha! No, I'm not the Devil, but I am the next best thing: I'm the puppeteer and yeah, I do enjoy you two empty heads belting the hell out of each other. So what are you's gonna do about it?"

The two trembling warriors turn to each other and continue to fight with even more gusto than before.

"I can't ...OOF! ... help it, Judy. There's ...OOF! ... something inside me that .... OFF! ... keeps driving me on to hit you."

"I can't ...OOF! ... help it either, Punch. I have no ...OOF! ... power over my own actions.

"Ha, Ha, Ha!" laughs the puppeteer. "This just gets better and better."

"Punch, we must ...OOF! ... pray to God for help – it's our only chance."

"Pray all that you want, my little featherweights. No one, not even God, can help you now."

"STOP RIGHT WHERE YOU ARE, PUPPETEER!"

"Who said that?"

"I SAID THAT."

"W... Where are you?" Wh.... Who are you?" A ... Are you God?"

"NO, PUPPETEER, I AM NOT GOD, BUT I AM THE NEXT BEST THING: I AM THE WRITER OF THIS STORY. AND YOU, MY FRIEND, ARE MY PUPPET."

"But I'm not a puppet, I'm a puppeteer!"

Punch and Judy clench themselves into boxing gloves and start bashing the puppeteer repeatedly on the head.

Left – Right – left and right.

Left – Right – left and right.

The puppeteer is unsteady on his feet.

Left – Right – Left, left and right.

He is swaying. He tries to steady himself on the stage, but Punch and Judy refuse to hold their punches. He collapses to the floor in a heap.

"We did it!" yell the happy puppets.

Tentatively, they disembowel the evil puppeteer from themselves and crawl away side by side into non-violent, zero-tolerant obscurity.

Plaster

Neither of us knew what love was before the accident. We were having sex at least once a day but it was more like a sporting event than anything else. Every guy at the party had been ogling her and it was doing my head in. At 2.30 a.m. I was well pissed and I ordered her to the car. Speeding along Helmer Avenue, she begged me to let her drive and that's when it happened.

I suffered mild concussion. Trish, on the other hand, was stuck in hospital for six months with multiple spinal injuries and a broken pelvis. She was encased in a plaster cast from her neck to her toes. If it hadn't been for Father Nichols, I would surely have committed suicide. He told me that I'd probably always have to carry some guilt with me but I could do a lot to make things up to her. When Trish left the hospital, she spent a further three months at home in her bedroom encased in plaster.

It was during her third week at home that her parents allowed me to visit her for the first time. I took along a plaster statuette of Christ on the cross to hang above her bed-head. She was genuinely grateful and told me the following week that it had given her extra strength.

Of course, everything was awkward to begin with. I knew that things would take time. Then, on my fifth visit, she asked me for a proper kiss and, though she couldn't move her head, it was the greatest kiss ever.

Since the accident, my mind had become focused entirely on Trish, other girls didn't interest me in the slightest. Something deep inside me had cracked and I knew that I would not enjoy sex again until she was out of that caste.

Trish told me that she'd been having erotic dreams about us. They involved us running across fields and swimming in the ocean. When I told her I'd been having identical dreams, she was ecstatic. She asked me to place my hand on her breast. The plaster was contoured to her form but was as hard as a rock.

As I ran my fingertips over the surface, she whispered that her nipple was hardening. I thought she was joking at first but then I discovered that I too could feel her warmth, her being, radiating through the plaster. I ran my hands the length of her body and, for the first time since the accident, I began to feel aroused.

From that day forward, I would spend hours at every visit just stroking her from top to toe. Never before had I felt so alive, so sensual, so in tune with another being. I wanted to crack that plaster open so badly I thought I would lose my mind.

When Trish told me that the nurses were coming the following morning to remove the caste, I was dumbstruck. I arrived at noon. As I walked up the front path, I noticed something protruding from the rubbish bin. It was the plaster caste. It had been neatly halved with cuts down both sides. With the utmost care, I lifted them out of the bin, carried them to my car and drove away, never to return.

True Colours

My bigoted work mates scoffed when I told them about Lisa and I. "I don't care what colour she is" I seethed, "I don't care if she's purple with green spots. I'm in love with her and that's all that matters to me!" It was my rostered day off but I couldn't keep away from her. She was my only friend in the world – the only one at work who always had a smile for me.

In all my years there, she'd only ever seen me in my grey security guard uniform. I thought it was about time to show her my true colours, so that morning I donned my carmine red trousers, a viridian green shirt with a flowing silk rainbow scarf and a magenta beret.

At 8.03 the Tuesday morning crowd oozed out of the tube and onto the platform, but that morning there was a single fleck of colour drifting along with the grey flow. Above the stencilled city skyline, a scheveningon red sun was rising through the sky. Cadmium orange blended with ultramarine blue right across the heavens – daubed with titanium white cloud.

I will admit to having a green streak in me and over the past three and a half years, I had become increasingly possessive of Lisa. Her being a model didn't help things; she was always the centre of attention. That morning, one young admirer stepped well over the mark, stirring up my deepest darkest emotions. I warned him to keep his distance but he just laughed in my face and brushed me aside. I was bristling with anger and I saw red – fiery, blinding alizarin red! With a lightning flourish, I whipped out my spatula and masterstroked him across the throat. Then, I saw even more red, trailing behind him, Jackson Pollock style, as he zigzagged away and slumped into still life. Then came the Muncheon screams – harrowing deafening – hands up to faces everywhere – swirling around the gallery and through my head. That's how I came to be locked in here.

I know she is the epitome of style and beauty. I know she is worth over two million quid. I know she was born in 1873. I know she is purple with green spots but I am a great believer in true love conquering every obstacle in its path.

Against All Odds

Father, I need to speak to you for a moment please.

Sure Jerry, what's on your mind, son?

It's my Christmas presents Father. You emphatically stated to me that it was Santa Claus who left my presents under the tree last night.

That's right, Boy.

Well Father, I went to the trouble of measuring my chemistry set and it's simply too wide to have passed through the chimney aperture.

Oh Son, sometimes old Santa has to use doors like everyone else when he's got extra big presents for the extra lucky boys and girls!

But Father, I took DNA samples off that glass of sherry that I left out for Santa last night and that DNA sample matches yours perfectly. The chances of someone other than you having drunken from that glass are 450 million to one. You have ruined my Christmas, Father, and you have completely destroyed my childhood. As a result, I phoned a solicitor this morning and I am going to sue you for £200,000 for your gross neglect in continuing to sustain my belief in Father Christmas.

But Jerry, you can't sue me: I'm not even your real father. You see Jerry, ten years ago when your mummy was working at the Women's prison, a prisoner gave her a baby because she didn't want the child adopted out to someone she didn't know – and that baby was you Jerry. Your mother and I were only too happy to go along with it because we couldn't have children ourselves.

You mean my real mother was a prisoner?

She *still is* a prisoner, Jerry. She's doing a very long sentence for stealing all those funds from the Children's Hospital Appeal – Oh don't cry, Jerry!

Well, who's my real daddy then?

He's in jail too, Son. He's very famous: you know the guy

who machetied all the penguins at the zoo?

You're just making all this up, you sicko!

I only wish I were making it up, Jerry. But after my wife – your surrogate mother – passed away, I got in touch with her best friend who still works at the prison. She managed to get a hold of DNA samples from both of your parents and they matched perfectly with yours I'm afraid. The chances of someone else, other than those two, being your parents are 625 million to one. Jerry! Jerry! Come back! Where are you going?

I – I – I'm going outside for a while – I want to be alone... Daddy! Daddy! Come out here quickly! QUICKLY!

W-What is it Jerry?

Look there in the grass!

It's dog shit Jerry.

No it's not Daddy. It's reindeer pooh! Santa Claus really WAS here last night after all!

No Jerry, that's just a dog turd , probably one of Rusty's – he's always crapping around here.

No Daddy, I know reindeer poohs when I see them, 'cos I saw some at the zoo last week!

We *could* do some D.N.A tests to make sure, Son.

No Daddy, I'm sure they're reindeers. Oh I'm so happy: Father Christmas really is true, isn't he!? And I'm the luckiest boy in the world to get that wonderful chemistry set. Merry Christmas DADDY! This is the best Christmas ever!

Merry Christmas Jerry, my boy.

Word Play

The curtain rises. Speaker One is seated centre stage in a bulky armchair. Beside him is a small table with a bowl of fruit. To the right of stage a cleaner is busy sweeping the floor. Speaker One jumps up out of his chair and tries to usher the cleaner off the stage.

Speaker One: Come on, get off the stage you fool, can't you see the curtains up?!

The cleaner refuses to budge an inch.

Cleaner: I don't care where the stupid curtain is, I'm paid to do the cleaning round here and that's what I'm doing.

Speaker One: But you can't do that now – the performance has begun for God's sake!

Cleaner: Look mate, normally, I clean back stage first and then do the stage at the end of my shift, but it just so happens that there's too much congestion out there at present – what with all that scenery and boxes of props in the way. So the only logical thing to do is start with the stage now and do back stage when all that stuff's been moved later on. I won't interfere with *your* job if you don't interfere with *mine* – look it's a big stage and there's plenty of room for everyone, so don't be so bloody selfish!

Speaker One: But this play is set in the seventeenth century – we can't have a cleaner wandering about in Adidas. Now get off!

Cleaner: But I'm an actor too!

Speaker One: No you're not: you're a cleaner. Now, get off stage or I'll have you sacked!!

Cleaner: But that's the sign of a great actor – that you can't tell I am in fact acting!

Speaker One: Listen to me – maybe you *are* an actor – maybe you're Laurence Olivia – but you don't belong up here right now because you're not written into the script, are you? And I don't recall seeing you at rehearsals except vacuuming the dressing rooms!

Cleaner: But I am written into the script and I *do* know my lines, and you're listening to them right *now*!

Speaker One: All right, all right. I'll prove that you're not in this play – I have a copy of the script backstage.

Speaker One marches off stage right, shaking his head.

Enter Stage Left: A man wearing an inkbottle costume and a woman dressed in an elaborate white paper dress. They hurry to centre stage, holding hands.

Cleaner: Now you two definitely weren't at rehearsals. The pantomime's on at the theatre next door. You both must have taken a wrong turn from your dressing rooms.

Mr Ink: You don't recognise us from the rehearsals because we weren't in costume. You'll no doubt remember us when you hear our recital. I'm Mr Ink! *(Takes a bow)*

Miss Paper: And I'm Miss Paper! *(Curtsies)*

Together: And we're here on centre page to recite the most contemporary poem ever written.

Cleaner: Excuse me – Don't you mean centre STAGE?!

Mr Ink: Centre Stage? You might like to *think* you're on Centre Stage you old drama queen, but I can assure you pal, we are at present on centre *page* – less than one per cent of all written plays ever make it onto the stage you know. Come on Miss Paper lets get this poem over and done with. We can still make it to the Crown and Anchor for last orders!

Miss Paper: *One word follows after the other!*
Mr Ink: *All strung out in lines!*
Miss Paper: *Lifting from some... INK and PAPER*
Mr Ink: *Wanders through the mind!*

Mr Ink bows ad Miss Paper curtsies. The cleaner claps his hands whilst leaning on his broom.

Cleaner: I didn't really understand it, but you were right: it did sound very contemporary. A bit abstract for my liking. Do you know any Wordsworth?

Miss Paper: Yes, you'll never hear anything as contemporary as that one!

Mr Ink: Yes, we like to write about what's happening right here and now, you know: how all the ink is spread across the paper; all shaped into words; the words getting identified through the readers eyes; the stage with all of us pouncing about; getting projected into the readers mind. Quite a clever little poem don't you think?

Cleaner: Are you trying to say we just exist in someone's mind?

Mr Ink: It's obvious, isn't it?

Miss Paper picks up an apple from the fruit bowl.

Cleaner: I wouldn't eat that if I were you, Love, it's made of wax – it's not real!

Miss Paper: I'm not real either – so it doesn't matter *(takes a big bite)*. You see, make-believe people are meant to eat make believe food, and real people are meant to eat real food, for instance. If I were to eat a real apple, I'd be just as sick as you would

	be if you were to eat this wax one. Each to their own, as they say!
Cleaner:	But it's wax, you fool!
Miss Paper:	*(chewing)* Yes, but have you ever seen such a shine and it's so crisp, hmmm!
Cleaner:	Don't go getting that wax all over the stage Love: if that gets trodden in, I'll have real problems getting that off.
Mr Ink:	Nothing here's real anyway. I wouldn't go to any real bother getting it clean, just go through the motions. That'll suffice.
Cleaner:	I do anyway Love, don't you worry about that! What with the wages they're paying me here!

Speaker One enters stage left and marches to centre stage holding a script. He looks at Mr Ink and Miss Paper in shock.

Speaker One:	Oh my God – now I've got *three* to get rid of! Listen to me all of you, I have with me the script for tonight's performance and there is absolutely no mention of a cleaner or a lady dressed in paper or an ink bottle with legs. Now, if you'll please just get off the stage!
Cleaner:	That's not a script; that's a prop! Sorry mate, but I think you've lost the plot completely.
Speaker One:	A prop hey? Well how come it says script on the front of it then?
Cleaner:	Because it's a good prop – the sign of a good prop is that you can't tell it from the real thing – like my acting! And furthermore, I saw it sitting in the prop box before I came on stage, which I might like to mention, was obstructing my cleaning areas around back stage.
Mr Ink:	*(To cleaner)* So is your acting just a part time hobby then?
Cleaner:	No! Acting is my full time job – it's as clean as a

whistle back stage. When I say it's still dirty out back, it's just my lines.

Speaker One: Listen, can you three idiots please discuss this outside – I've got a performance to put on!

Cleaner: Oh listen to the luvvie getting in a tizz!

Mr Ink: Yeah, calm down Drama Queen, we're all only a figment in some reader's petty little mind anyway!

Speaker One charges off stage left.

Cleaner: (Yelling after Speaker One). You've gone the wrong way – the prop box is this side (pointing to stage right).

Speaker One charges from stage left across stage – exits stage right.

Cleaner: (Turns to Mr Ink and Miss Paper). Typical actor, isn't he? Getting all flustered.

The three of them laugh together.

Speaker One enters stage right clutching a can of petrol and a lit cigarette lighter.

Speaker One: Figments, eh? Just little figments in someone's petty little mind, eh? Well how come you're all looking a trifle worried now then?

Miss Paper: It's not us we're worried about; it's the readers' brain that's at stake here!

The Cleaner points to the two fire exits either side of the stage.

Cleaner: Ink and Paper, quickly, I'm sure there's a fire extinguisher down one of those fire exits!

Mr Ink and Miss Paper jump off the stage. Miss Paper exits fire exit left. Mr Ink exits fire exit right.

Cleaner: Don't be a fool, Speaker One. You're the star of the show. Don't let your career go up in smoke. Just hand me the can of petrol and I'll get off the stage!

Speaker One starts tipping the fuel all over the stage.

Speaker One: Little figments eh? Just little tiny figments? Ha! Ha! Ha!

Miss Paper re-appears at the fire exit left.

Miss Paper: There's no extinguisher down there and it stinks of earwax!

Mr Ink re-appears at fire exit right.

Mr Ink: I couldn't find any fire extinguisher. It smells like earwax down there and it's slippery under foot!

Cleaner: All right! I didn't get a chance to mop there yet; too busy arguing up here, wasn't I?

Speaker One throws the cigarette lighter onto the stage – flames shoot up everywhere.

Cleaner: I know what to do!

The Cleaner climbs up the curtain at stage left, pulls a large knife from his back pocket.

Cleaner: (*Yelling to Speaker One*). You see this knife? I told you I wasn't really a cleaner!

The Cleaner starts cutting away at the curtain. The whole thing falls down – falling completely flat over the stage. As flat as a piece of paper from a script. Only Mr Ink and Miss Paper remain.

THE END

Off The Rails

Tickets, please! *Tickets, please!* May I see your ticket, please madam?

Mr Cromwell, listen to me. You are *not* a ticket man and we are *not* on a train. We're in Section B of the Aspley Acres Psychiatric Hospital.

May I see your ticket, please madam?

Mr Cromwell, will you get back to your bed! Don't you know where you are? You're in hospital, remember?

Madam, will you just show me your ticket, please, and I'll be on my way. I've got another three carriages to inspect.

Mr Cromwell, if you're a ticket man, how come I know your name?

Well, madam, it does say "Bernard Cromwell" right here on my badge, doesn't it?

For God's sake, Mr Cromwell, look out the window. Do you see trees and fields whizzing past?

Of course there's no trees or fields whizzing past, we're passing through the Glenbervie Industrial Estate. Madam, if you're not going to produce a valid ticket or offer to buy one, I shall be forced to issue an on-the-spot fine — do you understand what I'm saying?

All right, all right, Mr Cromwell. I'll have a ticket from the last station to the next one, OK? And make that a one-way ticket!

Madam, you didn't get on at the last station, did you? I looked out the door at the last station and nobody got on at all.

Listen, Mr Cromwell, I didn't get on any bloody train. I entered this ward half an hour ago to keep an eye on you — that's why I'm wearing this nurse's uniform. I am a *nurse* and you are a *patient*! Now will you please get back to your bed! I have a *hell* of a headache!

Madam, I don't care what profession you're in. All passengers must produce a valid ticket or be prepared to purchase a ticket.

All right, all right, all right, just give me a ticket — a valid ticket — from anywhere to anywhere, if you promise just to leave me in peace and get back to your bed. God, I don't know why I'm doing this stupid job. I should have stuck it out on the production line at Kellogg's — at least I worked decent shifts and went home at the end of the day with peace of mind.

Madam, don't cry — please don't cry. It's not that important. We'll forget about your fare this time — you can pay on your next journey, all right?

Mr Cromwell, it's eleven o'clock now and that's the end of my shift. I shall see you again tomorrow morning at six-thirty.

Madam, where are you going? Get away from that door! This train is moving at eighty miles per hour — you'll be killed instantly!

Oh shit, Mr Cromwell, where's the next station then?

We'll be coming into Chelmer station in approximately four minutes and I'm going to sit right here with you to make sure you don't do anything silly.

Mr Cromwell, I've got kids to put to bed. It's the end of my shift. I'll miss my train!

How can you miss your train when you're already on the damned thing? Listen to me, young lady, are you getting enough sleep? Are you eating sensibly?

No, I'm bloody well not eating sensibly and I sleep two hours per night and this job is doing my bloody *head* in!

Do you have someone at home, pet, who can take care of you?

Yeah, I've got a husband, if you can call him that. He thinks I'm his bloody servant.

There, there, madam — here, take my handkerchief. Shall we phone him on my mobile so he can meet you at the station?

That's a laugh! He wouldn't get off his arse for me. Do you know what he called me last night in front of his mates? — His Baby Elephant!

Ah, I see your problem now, madam. Let me guess: You help yourself to a bit of amphetamine at work to lose weight, because you're sick of not measuring up to those matchstick women in those stupid magazines — am I right?

Well, I *have* taken speed a *few* times, just to keep myself going.

You see, pet, that's why you think you're still at work — you've dozed off here on the train and you've mixed things up in your head, haven't you? Look, we're coming into Chelmer station now. Let me help you onto the platform, you silly thing!

*As Nurse Sanders fell from the sixth-storey window there followed a shrill cry of "**Mind the gap**!"*

Hi Bloody Ho!

Tonight, Larry, is your big night! Tonight, I'm giving you Andy's job on a silver platter! You've been playing Sneezy now for over two years and it's time you had a shot as the lead dwarf. I know it's short notice, Larry, but I know you can do it. You've been doing the show long enough to know everyone's lines, and I think you'll make a brilliant Happy!

But Tom, *Happy* isn't the leading dwarf!

He is tonight, Larry.

But, if I've got Andy's job, who's Andy playing then?

That's the other thing I have to tell you about, Larry. Andy has left the show – he's outta town. Let's face it, Larry, his heart wasn't in it anymore.

But Tom, we all lost heart because we're doing three shows a day, seven days a week for peanuts – that's why Andy's left!

Oh come off it Larry. You can see yourself: we're not getting full houses anymore. How can I give you guys' full wages when the cash isn't coming in? There's nothing that'd please me more than giving you all a good pay rise!

But we've all lost heart because we all feel exploited. Just because we're half everyone else's size doesn't mean we should get half everyone else's wages!

Oh don't start that Union shit again Larry. Who's gonna feed your wife and kids if you lose this job, hey? I'm not trying to be cruel, Larry; I'm just telling you how it is. Who's gonna hire a dishwasher who can't see over a sink? Think about it Larry! Times are tough right now. We're operating on a razor thin profit margin and the accountant has told me the wages can't be increased until we start getting arses on seats.

But Tom, how come you're driving round town in a brand new Mercedes Benz?

Oh Larry, listen to me pal, that's just a tax dodge – buying that car. Now hold still Larry while I get this rouge on your cheeks. We haven't got long before curtain time and we've got some new fellas coming round that we need to brief before the show. And don't give me that long face Larry, I know you're just trying to make me feel guilty.

New fellas?

Yeah, Larry, the other dwarves followed Andy out the door today - they wouldn't listen to common sense - so I'm borrowing some midgets from Billington's Circus to fill in, just until we get some more staff. Tonight we're gonna have to improvise a fair bit. But I'm counting on you Larry to lead 'em all through the routine. I know you can do it. I'm counting on you Larry!

Oh shit Tom – you mean they've ALL walked out? That's it – I'm leaving right now!

Don't talk Larry. I'm trying to draw your mouth nice and wide.

But it's ridiculous Tom – let's face it – the show's washed up!

Calm down, Larry – I don't want these new boys to hear you talking like that! You're gonna save the show tonight Larry: you're gonna lead those new boys out there and knock em dead – do you hear me? Now, don't move while I draw this big smile on your face – Ah! – There! – See – Look in the mirror Larry! Things are looking better already!

Of Mouse and Man

Ladies and gentlemen, my next guest has been a household name in the cartoon world for longer than anyone can remember. Recently, he has turned his talents to rock 'n' roll and he is here in Britain, for the very first time, to promote his début single, a cover version of Elvis Presley's *Caught in a Trap*, ladies and gentlemen — the one and only, Mister Dickie Mouse!

Hi, everyone!

So, Mister Mouse —

Please Rob, call me Dickie.

OK, Dickie, welcome to Vermin Radio! You've been appearing at Eurodizzy in France for the past decade. Why has it taken you so long to come to Britain?

Golly, Rob, are you a dummy or something? The Dickie Mouse at Eurodizzy is just some college kid in a mouse costume!

Ha-ha! You're taking the Mickie, Dickie! Actually, Dickie, I was just noticing *your* outfit and I must say I *am* impressed — is it some sort of new material? It's *so* convincing.

Convincing? *Convincing?* I'll have you know, young man, that this suit was tailor made for me by George Armani himself, tailor made for my *tail* to poke through at the back! Ha-ha! Times are tough, Rob, but Dickie Mouse doesn't need to wear imitation quality — no sirree!

Actually, Dickie, I was referring to the mouse suit *between* you and the Armani. It looks *so* convincing compared to the Eurodizzy Dickie.

Rob, wake up and smell the cheese, pal! I'm not just some bloke inside a mouse suit!

A woman, then?

It is attitudes like yours, Rob, that make my life so difficult. Just because I've been with Walt Dizzy for a long time, you can't accept the fact that Dickie Mouse has other talents in other fields. Look at Madonna, Whitney Houston, Britney Spears, Barbara

Streisand: they've all made the transition from singing to acting. You yourself, Rob, have changed from short story writing to working on radio. Why is it so hard to accept that Dickie Mouse is breaking out of the cartoon world into rock 'n' roll?

Dickie, the notion of changing from singer to actor is a hell of a lot more plausible than a cartoon character all of a sudden becoming a *real* rock 'n' roll star!

We'll see about that, Rob. My first record 'Caught in a Trap' is currently Number 7 in the charts *with* a bullet!

Yeah, yeah, Dickie, but listen to me —

Go ahead, Rob, I'm all ears.

Let's face it, Dickie, you're the first guest I've ever had on this show who doesn't have a history of sexual indiscretions or drug problems; the only thing *you* have in *your* closet is that state of the art mouse outfit! Cartoon characters ARE NOT and NEVER CAN BE real. They don't even have their own thoughts and they don't even really move: it's just thousands of little drawings flickering through a projector.

Oh, listen to Mister "I Think, Therefore I Am, and You Don't, Therefore You Aren't" speaking! It must be hard work for you, Rob, having to keep thinking that you are real all the time. Do you get days off?

No, Dickie, I don't get days off, but I don't *have to* keep thinking that I'm real *all* of the time. I've got other things I have to think about as well.

So, Rob, while you're thinking about other things, you are no longer thinking about yourself?

Yes.

So when you are thinking that I'm *not* real, you are no longer thinking that you *are* real?

Well, Dickie, I can only think about one thing at once, can't I?

Sounds to me, Rob, like we're in the same boat! I need thousands of little drawings flickering through a projector to exist and you need thousands of little thoughts projected through your head to exist. Face up to it, Rob! What are you: a mouse or a man?

Dickie, I'm afraid that's all we have time for this morning. I think I could do with a drink right now, so, will you be out clubbing tonight then, Dickie?

Shucks no, Rob, I've got my own club back in the States with over half a million members. I could do with a vacation from clubs for a while, I can tell you!

Dickie, one thing before you scurry off: do you think I might have a future in the cartoon world?

Bonkers

God blimey mate, gimme room. Let me sit down! You wouldn't believe the shit I've been through tonight. - It's a bloody miracle I'm still alive. Started off in Bunker 7 – me and this bloke named Ronnie. We were under fire all day. The Gerry's crept up to within forty yards of us – but we stood our ground and they eventually retreated. Then as the sun was goin' down, I showed him a photo of Marie, my sweetheart back home. Ronnie tells me she's a lovely looking girl then he says "As we've been through so much together, I'd like to let you in on a secret". So he pulls out a photo of his sweetheart who's also in the forces: a guy named Herbert. Jesus, I nearly chucked up on the spot. I'd spent the whole day with a Nancy boy without even knowing it! A man can't even fight for his own country without getting stuck in a bunker with a queer. I ran out of there so fast, I left me rifle and ammo behind.

I nearly had me head shot off before I found Bunker 6, but when I get in there, there's a fist fight goin on. I'm trying to work out which one's the Gerry, but they're both *our* boys! It seems one of 'em was a Protestant and the other was a Catholic and after coming under fire, they both went to pray and it just kicked off from there. I tried to break 'em up, but I was too exhausted so I up and left.

By this time, it's pitch black – must have taken me half an hour to find Bunker 5. I gets in there and I'm telling this bloke named Albert me tale of woe, then he goes to light a fag and would you believe it, he's a darkie! Jesus Christ! The reason I'm fightin' for my county is to keep the likes of him OUT. I was so disgusted, I risked life and limb getting to Bunker 4, me clothes in tatters.

I get talking to a geezer named Barry – we were talking for about an hour – getting on really well, then he brings up the subject of what he's gonna do when he gets home. Says he can't wait to see Stanthorpe United play again and would you believe it: I'm a Williamstown Blues supporter!

Everyone knows they're old rivals from WAY back. I'd been

in countless punch-ups with the likes of his sort, so rather than waste any more energy I decided to get out of there, quick smart!

But this time, I'm thrown sky high by a hand grenade and I don't know where the hell I'm runnin'. All I know is to just keep the hell movin'. It was pure luck I found this Bunker. It's a sad day for Britain when a man can't even fight for his country beside a man he can trust! You don't come under any of those categories do you mate? 'Cos I haven't got the strength to keep running!

Nein, Ich habe reinlich blut. Ich bin ein Nazi!

Reality T.V.

The Ruben family loved reality T.V. and the realer it got, the more they loved it. Who needs Eastenders, Coronation Street, Neighbours or Home and Away when you can see the real thing? They loved real interaction, real passion, real arguments, and real love.

Sure, the storylines took longer to develop and weren't as spectacular as the soaps, but the Ruben family felt that it was well worth the wait.

One night, Mister Ruben went to turn the television on and something popped inside the set. All eyes followed a tiny wisp of smoke to the ceiling, then the family gazed in disbelief into their own long reflections in the vacant screen.

The Big Picture

"Come over here into the corner Karen, so we can talk privately" whispered Doctor Barkley. He then pinned Nurse Stewart against the bed and gasped, "You know I'll always love you, Karen, and we're going to be together forever and ever as soon as my divorce comes through."

Yesterday he had done exactly the same thing to Nurse Baxter.

"Please Karen, one little kiss to help me through the day!"

Nurse Stewart wriggled away and snapped "Michael, have a bit of respect for poor Mister Rickard here!"

The Doctor laughed "Mister Rickard's been in a coma for the past three years!"

"It doesn't matter, Michael it's unprofessional, and you'll just have to wait until tomorrow night for a kiss you naughty boy!"

Five minutes later Roger the porter came whistling into the ward. He sidled up to Nurse Stewart who was busy pushing buttons on the life support machine.

"Close your eyes and stick out your ring finger!" he demanded "No peeking – I said *no* peeking".

"Oh Roger, it's gorgeous!" She shrieked. "But you can't afford this!"

"I refuse to have my future wife wearing trash!" he announced proudly.

Half an hour later Nurse Stewart called Nurse Baxter into the ward "Can you help me with this Life Support Unit, Dianne, I've got a problem with it!" When she came through Nurse Stewart whispered "There's nothing wrong with it, I just had to tell you that what happened between us last night was FANTASTIC – that was my first lesbian experience and I've just got to see you again tonight – can you come around at about 8?"

"Sure, I'll be looking forward to it!" whispered Nurse Baxter, before striding out again.

Sometimes I wonder if half the goings on around this bed is nothing but a little drama created by my own mind. To tell the truth, I don't care if it's real or not, just as long as it's entertaining! I might have one foot in and one foot out of a coma, but does anybody anywhere really know what's real and what's not? Sometimes I ask myself: if I'm just a vegetable, who is unable to do anything for itself, am I still an actual human being? But then I think "vegetable" and "human being" are only labels aren't they? I am what I am. Who cares? But there is one thing that *I do know* for sure and that is that *I am the consciousness of this ward*! All the characters that come and go through here think that I am just a piece of meat who knows nothing and hears nothing, but, because they hold this misconception, I get to know more about everyone than anybody else alive! Although I can't lift my eyelids, I do get to see the big picture. Ha! Maybe I am God? But any which way I look at it, life doesn't get much better than this!

The Ultimate High

The plan was to get as far away from the housing scheme as we could with a bundle of cash and tons of drugs to last us a few weeks.

Heading up the Highway in the stolen Shogun – we had it made – we were smoking joints as fast as I could roll them and, just when we thought we couldn't get any higher, Lenny pulls the crack pipe out from under the seat. God knows how he kept control of that car – I swear we were floating three feet above the road. Then, to top it off, Shalina starts dropping acid tabs onto our tongues like she's some kind of high priestess. As we were leaving civilisation well and truly behind us, we were also getting well and truly out of our own skulls.

In the middle of nowhere, we came across this crappy little farmhouse. Lenny didn't stop the car – we just smashed straight through the gates. A dog ran uot barking, so I pulled out my handgun and blew it away. Lenny was well impressed.

"That's what I like about the countryside" he said. "You can do what you want and nobody bothers you!"

Lenny kicked in the front door of the house and the three of us barged in but no one was home. I looked out the back and found an old bugger working in the veggie patch. I picked up a shovel and snuck up behind him. He was on his knees in the dirt taking little plants out of a box and planting them all in a line. The first hit sent his hat and hearing aid flying and he just crumpled in a heap. I remember wincing at his filthy hands and body odour. I thought I was doing the old bastard a favour, I mean, he must have had his last shag twenty years ago, and what's the use in carrying on, if you've got no mates and you spend your whole life fucking about in a shitty little veggie patch?

I stuck his skanky hat on my head and the three of us carried him out to the back paddock, then I put his old green wellies on and danced about – the other two were choking with laughter. I remember Shalina spinning around and around, singing out that we could live there forever and ever. Lenny shagged her in the barn, then I shagged her in the veggie patch. Lenny found a rifle in the house and took Shalina on safari, shooting chickens and cows and shit.

Without thinking, I knelt down where the old man had been working and continued planting all the seedlings in the furrowed earth. By this time, I'm starting to feel fucking higher than I've ever been before: like I'm still in my body but I'm looking down on it too and my hands are looking really old and callused. I start seeing all these little plants in a way I've never seen them before: each one was a perfect little creation of the universe; each one belonged there in its own space. Even the weeds were fucking brilliant and every little drop of water on every little leaf was like a million-pound jewel, containing the whole universe. There was no yesterday, no tomorrow, just the earth and the plants and the heavens and me and everything was like perfect. When I stuck my hands in the fresh soil, I could smell the earth like never before. I had no problems anymore: anyone could have called me a bastard and I wouldn't have even bothered reacting! I had found the ultimate high.

Then, I got transfixed on this one big red tomato: it was so perfect and shiny that, when I looked up close, I could see my own reflection in it, only it wasn't my face looking back out at me, but that of the old man. As I looked even closer, I could see someone sneaking up behind him wielding a shovel.

The Phantom Of The Soap Opera

You might well ask what an old bloke like me is doing cleaning offices from 10p.m. to 6.30 a.m., Monday to Saturday. You're probably wondering 'What about his family? What about his social life?' Fact is, I lost my wife and two kids years ago when I did a long stretch for safe cracking and forging art treasures. And as for my social life, nowadays, I know better than to keep company with my old business colleagues and inmates, as it would only be a matter of time before I was back in the can! I started off on the day shift with this cleaning firm, but I couldn't stand all the back-stabbing and every bastard trying to crawl up the boss's arse, so the night shift was my only answer. And as for my sex drive, that flopped right alongside my art career!

At least don't get any hassles with this little job. I just get the work done, go back to my bedsit, feed Vincent – my goldfish, watch television, walk in the park, sleep, wake up, eat and go back to work again. Simple!

It might sound weird but I do look upon some of the people who work in this building as my family and I can still feel their presence here hours after they've left the premises. I know what everyone looks like because of all the photo's stuck everywhere. Then we have all the Birthday cards, Valentine cards, Christmas cards, Engagements, Weddings, office memos – then there was the funeral – that's when I finally got to see everyone in real life – but I'll get to that! What I'm trying to say is that all these cards and things help to keep me informed of what's happening like a very close yet distant relative who doesn't exist!

Having been in the forging business for thirty odd years, you get a very keen eye for detail. I can tell a hell of a lot about a person by their handwriting. Then there are all those toys and artefacts everyone likes to keep on top of their computers – these are perfect little displays of the owner's inner self. But the very best source of information comes directly from the waste paper baskets. The waste paper basket is a treasure throve of intimate communications between the daytime ghosts that are my family, friends and enemies.

Notes that have been torn into a thousand pieces are always personal as opposed to the screwed up variety and are worth every hour of reconstruction back in my lonely little bedsit.

Janet Moulard – the junior secretary, who is the mother of my son, doesn't even know I exist. She doesn't know that there is someone who looks forward to seeing the photographs of her smiling face six nights a week. She's not the kind of girl who would stand out in a crowd but she has a subtle beauty that grew on me slowly and steadily, and before I knew it, I was infatuated. She's the only one in the whole god damned building who writes 'please' on her lunch order too. I'm not sure about all those new age books she reads but I do know her heart's in the right place.

I know what you're thinking right now, though. How does an old bloke with no sex life, father a child to a woman that he's hardly even met before? Artificial insemination? No. Let's say it was just a little bit of divine intervention on my part that ushered Charles Junior into the world of the living.

It all started just over two years ago. Janet was going through a rough patch in her personal life. Love letters and poems written by her started to appear in some of the guy's baskets around the building. Then she started comfort eating – amongst all the tissues in her basket, I'd find five, six, sometimes seven chocolate wrappers a day! This would go on for a month or so, then we'd have a week of low fat yoghurt containers followed by another month of chocolate, chocolate, chocolate! I started to really worry when the Prozac packets appeared. Sometimes, I wished that I could just give her a big hug, but all I could ever manage was what one of her new age books described as a 'mental hug'.

The love letters came to light between her and Rick Peterson, the Deputy Manager. She thought she'd found the love of her life, but if she'd seen Peterson's stash of illegal porn in his safe and his explicit correspondence to some of the other secretaries around the building, she wouldn't have been so love struck, I can tell you!

Then, one day, I found a pregnancy test packet in her basket! I ran to the ladies loo and there, at the bottom of the bin, was the tester and it showed POSITIVE! You could have knocked me over with a feather! Not much vacuuming got done that night, I can tell you. I was too busy pacing up and down and searching for a Prozac to calm my nerves. I didn't sleep a wink when I got home and the following night's discoveries were even more alarming. First, I pieced together a torn-up note from Peterson to Janet saying that he could never leave his wife and kids, and that she'd have to have an abortion. Then I pieced together a half-written suicide note by Janet saying that she couldn't go on living – feeling so rejected. I poured myself a long whiskey from Peterson's office and went to the boardroom to think.

'Rejected' was the word in her note that kept jumping out at me – it'd be easy enough for me to send her some of the notes that he'd sent to some of the other secretaries but that would only enhance her feelings of rejection. So, using my old talent for forging, I wrote a letter to Janet in Peterson's hand on his personalised notepaper, saying that he'd changed his mind and that he was going to leave his wife and kids to set up a new home with Janet. I also wrote that if the child was a boy, he wanted it to be called Charles, after a distant Uncle of his from Sunderland who he had admired as a child. I placed the note in Janet's top drawer then went home to fetch some of my own notepaper.

I wrote a series of threatening letters to Peterson demanding huge cash repayments, and then I placed these letters in his safe, after emptying it of pornography and other valuables. Peterson didn't arrive at work that morning. His car was found in a lay-by five miles out of town. He'd been murdered with a single shot to the back of the head. I didn't get any vacuuming done that night.

It was a marvellous funeral; everyone dressed in the colour of night. All those two-dimensional faces actually coming to life! As they were lowering the coffin, I was standing at the back of the crowd, squinting in the mid-day sunshine and wiping imaginary tears away, when I became aware of a small figure sobbing beside me. It was Janet! Before I knew it, I'd put my arm around her and, to my surprise, she cuddled in close to me. When the crowd were dispersing, I introduced myself as Charles Peterson. Janet gave me an actual real life hug that will warm my bones till my dying day, then she feigned indifference and walked away!

    The day shift cleaners were right when they said you can get away with murder on the night shift! Yesterday, I found a note in the manager's bin from Janet apologising for being two hours late in for work – apparently, Charles Junior had kept her up half the night. If that isn't a chip off the old block: sounds like the boy's a natural for the night shift!

Mobius Dick

I am all alone in the waiting room, clutching my seat for dear life whilst my body flails around in mid air. I am the only thing here that gravity is playing havoc with. In my back pocket is a big plastic tag with the number one marked on it. A buzzer sounds and I see that the number 'one' is illuminated in red above the reception desk. The receptionist lifts her head from the desk and drones through the glass partition. "Doctor Escher will see you now, Mister Dick." I let go of my seat and a centrifugal force throws me against the wall. I slide along towards her, four feet above the floor. The side of my face squashes up against the glass. I grip the hole in the glass to stop myself being swept away. "Your number tag, please" she asks blandly. With my free hand I manage to pass the tag through the hole and I notice that her appointment book is filled with my name and my name only. She lowers her head back down on her desk as the invisible whirlpool sends me tumbling along the corridor wall and straight through Doctor Escher's Doorway.

I manage to grab a hold of the door handle and my body wavers around his office like a windsock in a storm. "Why are your eyes bulging so much Mister Dick?" asks Doctor Escher, calmly. I am gulping for air "Because I am half man and half gold fish!" "I see", replies the Doctor, whilst searching through his notes. "During our last appointment, Mister Dick, which was – let me see now – twenty minutes ago – I handed you some medication to take – did you follow my directions Mister Dick? I shrug my non existant shoulders " I can't quite remember Doctor Escher" He looks up from his notes and takes his spectacles off "I Keep telling you, don't I, Mister Dick, if you don't take your medication you'll never step out of this cycle!" He opens his cupboard, there are thousands of jars, all with my name printed neatly on the labels.

He grabs me by the knee to hold me still as he places one of the jars in my pocket. He writes something in his notes. The invisible whirlpool is beginning to wind down a bit and I stand almost normally upon the floor. "Please remember to take your medication Mister Dick and I shall see you again at our next appointment, take care now, Goodbye!" The world swims around me as I squelch back to the reception. The receptionist raises her head from her desk "shall I slot you in for the next appointment Mister Dick?" "The next appointment?" I ask "Why would I want to book the next appointment as well?" "It's what you always do Mister Dick" She wearily hands me the plastic tag with number one marked on it "Please take a seat, when you hear the buzzer and your number appears on the display, return the disc to me and go through to Doctor Escher's room, which is the first door on the right" She smiles weakly and gently places her head back down on her desk.

    I pirouette to the centre of the waiting room. The Gold fish is pirouetting in the centre of his bowl. As always, I pour my medication in, then with the big plastic tag, I stir vigorously.

Finding The Words

Years ago, he had a fine vocabulary but, nowadays, he is finding it increasingly difficult to find the right words to express himself. By the time he has remembered the word on the tip of his tongue, he has forgotten the context into which he was intending to use it.

"Look at the lovely chocolates Auntie Mable has sent you Dad."

He eyes the chocolates beside his bed. He doubts if he will ever be well enough to eat again.

"Tell A-Auntie – Auntie? – Th – thank her for me!"

She squeezes his hand, trying to inject some of her life force into him. A tear rolls off her cheek.

"Sharon, you're the best – the best – the? –"

Now, not only do the words escape him, but he has also lost the capacity to engage his thoughts with the muscles in his mouth.

"It's all right, Dad, I know what you mean!"

He manages a faint smile as his eyelids gently fall. She continues to speak to him, but words no longer exist, there is only warm sound. She squeezes his hand and the eyelids lift to reveal the most beautiful smile he has ever seen. He no longer even knows this person seated before him – he no longer knows anything. The eyelids fall as he drifts into infinity.

Over the next couple of months he sleeps a great deal and although he is mute and bedridden, he sees the world with newfound wonder. His most regular visitor who feeds him and speaks the warmest sound in the world always seems to know what he is trying to communicate.

As the months roll by there are lots of tears, but lots of laughter too.

One day whilst gazing into her lovely face and squeezing her outstretched finger, something amazing happens. Completely out of nowhere a word comes to mind and, out of nowhere, he also finds the ability to engage that word with his tongue. As naturally as a starling taking flight or a bud opening in spring, he gurgles "mamma".

Left On The Shelf

Just when I thought I had closed an unhappy chapter in my life, she saunters back into the Clayton Library as if it was her first visit. For five and a half years, we'd had a close friendship working there together and then, we became lovers and she just lost the plot completely.

Now here she was, without her spectacles, in a ridiculous modern outfit, squinting around the Romance Section.

"Pardon me, Madam," I enquired, "is there a particular book or a particular person I can help you locate?"

"Stanley! You gave me a fright! How are you? – it's been a long time."

"Yes, Maxine, your return is three months overdue. I'm afraid you've accumulated a thousand pound fine."

Though she had a new hairstyle, she twirled her hair the way she always did.

"Am I worth that much, Stanley?"

"Do you still read poetry, Max?" I asked excitedly.

"No, not since I've been single." She looked at the bookshelf.

"Come over to Poetry. We've finally got the Love Poems of John Donne on our shelves!"

"I'll wait here Stan. You get the book."

I rushed over to the Poetry Section, grabbed the book and dashed back to Romance, but she was nowhere to be seen. I started scanning the aisles for her. It was whilst passing through History that something caught the corner of my eye. I moved toward the shelf and peered through the books into the Horror Section. There was Maxine in the arms of Adam Siddall, my new co-worker. Not only had he re-arranged every square inch of the Library to make it more user-friendly, computerised everything that could be computerised, he moves in on my ex-girlfriend just to rub my nose right into it.

The poetry book fell to the floor, as I wandered dejectedly to the Philosophy Section. I sat in there on a footstool with my chin on my fist. "Why me?" I kept asking myself. "Why am I here anyway? What does it all mean?"

Just then, Maxine walked alone into the Fiction Section and I cornered her. "So, you've come here to see Adam and wind me up – is that your game?"

"That's rubbish, Stan. Adam and I are just good friends." She pushed past me and slipped into the Non Fiction Section.

"Stanley, please stop following me – OK, if it makes you feel happy, we are seeing each other, OK? It's all over between us, Stan, I thought you would have found someone else by now!"

She ran to the end of the Non Fiction aisle and turned left into Law.

"Stanley, I said stop following me. I could get you charged with stalking, you know!"

"Maxine, don't fucking even turn up at this Library again. I know you're just trying to fuck with my feelings!"

"Stan, this Library is a PUBLIC PLACE and I have every right to visit here whenever it takes my fancy, and, if you swear at me once more, I'll have you up for indecent behaviour!"

She made her way into Entertainment. "Stanley, stop following me. Look, you're making a big scene. The whole Library is watching us!"

"Alright, Maxine, let's just sort this out quietly in the corner, OK?"

"What? In the Crime Section?"

"Yeah, we can be alone in there."

As we passed my desk, I slipped my steel letter opener into my back pocket.

Real Trouble

The Unicorn was telling the Goblin that Goblins were nothing but fictitious beings from fictitious stories. The Goblin countered that Unicorns were nothing but faerie creatures from faerie tales. The argument was growing more and more serious, so I stepped in.

"Listen to me, both of you! You're both make-believe characters, so stop the arguing — it's ridiculous!"

The two of them stared at me in amazement; then they broke into laughter.

"Look who's calling who 'make-believe'!" shouted the Goblin. "A Human Being of all creatures!"

The pair fell about in hysterics.

I stood my ground.

"You two have been part of the make-believe world for hundreds of years on Earth. The person who invented you, Mister Goblin, probably just said, 'I know, I'll create a little man with a big nose and long feet — the children will find that amusing!' And as for you, Mister Unicorn, someone just looked at a horse and thought: I know, I'll put a horn on its head and call it a Unicorn; that'll be different."

The Unicorn burst into tears.

"It can't be true — it can't be true. I don't want to be a make-believe thing!"

"Don't take it so bad, Mister Unicorn," I offered. "You look just like a horse, except for that horn on your head, and everyone on Earth loves horses; they're beautiful creatures."

"I AM a horse anyway," said the Unicorn indignantly. "I just stuck this horn on my head for a laugh."

"But, Mister Unicorn, horses can't speak at all, and you seem to have a fine vocabulary."

The Unicorn looked at me dumbly, pretending that it couldn't understand a word.

The Goblin put his hands on his hips.

"Well, you might be pleased to know, Mister Human, that where I come from Human Beings have always been favourite creatures in our popular fantasy. Ages ago, a Goblin writer just thought: What I need is a tall, featureless being with a button nose that can walk around thinking that it has a monopoly of reality!"

The Goblin gestured to me with an open palm as if to say, "Here is the evidence!" Then he continued, in a condescending tone:

"So, Mister Reality, DO tell us all about yourself."

I proudly tapped my chest with my thumb and announced:

"I am from the real world — I live on Planet Earth."

The Goblin eyed me suspiciously.

"And what exactly is a planet?"

I stretched my arms out as wide as I could.

"It's like a huge ball, and it turns around, and humans like me live all around the surface of it."

"Oh, do you now, Mister Human? And how come you don't all get squashed when this big ball rolls around?" he mocked.

"Because the ball doesn't sit on anything. It turns through empty space."

"Empty space?" bellowed the Goblin. "I've seen EMPTY pots and I've seen EMPTY pockets, but I must say I've NEVER seen EMPTY space. DO tell us about EMPTY space, Mister Reality, please DO!"

"Well, there's empty space between you and me, isn't there?"

The Unicorn suddenly found his voice again.

"No, not at all. From where you're standing there is a space and then there's the Goblin, and from where the Goblin is standing there is a space and then there's you — but that's not EMPTY space. Please DO tell us about this empty space, Mister Human."

I took a deep breath.

"There is space and then there's more space and then there is more and more and more space."

The Goblin elbowed the Unicorn.

"He's making it up as he goes along!"

Then they danced around chanting:

"There's more space and more space and more and more and more space." The Goblin added: "He's got EMPTY SPACE between his ears!"

The Unicorn whinnied.

"Let's not be too hard on the poor fellow. After all, he's only HUMAN!"

The nasty pair could hardly stand up, they laughed so loud.

I pointed to the Goblin.

"All right, Mister know-all. If you're so smart, tell us all about the place you're from then."

"Where I'm from?" answered the Goblin gravely. "Where I'm from, there is no space at all, just dirt and sand and rocks everywhere."

"But that's impossible! If there was nothing but dirt and sand and rocks, nobody could even move around, could they?"

The Goblin shook his head slowly.

"Things are tough in the REAL WORLD."

"That's a pathetic explanation!" I protested. "What's OUTSIDE all this dirt and sand and rocks then?"

"Just rock," he shrugged.

"Well, what's outside all the rock then?"

The Goblin clenched his fist.

"It is SOLID ROCK!"

I turned to the Unicorn.

"Can you believe that? And he has the cheek to laugh at MY WORLD. That's the most outrageous, illogical thing I've ever heard in my life!"

The Unicorn pointed to me with his horn.

"There's more foundation to the Goblin's story than there is to your 'more space and more space, etc., etc., etc.' story!"

My mouth fell open wide.

"I know what to do!" yelled the Goblin. "We'll settle this like adults — we'll take a vote on who thinks who is real!" Then he leaned over to me. "I'll vote for you, if you vote for me!"

"Grow up!" I screamed.

"Hands up," commanded the Goblin, "those of you who think Goblins are real creatures!"

The Goblin's hand shot up, while the Unicorn and I looked around nonchalantly.

"That's one vote for the Goblins," said the Goblin. "Now, who thinks that Humans are real creatures?"

I slowly raised my hand, whilst trying to work out the logic of this exercise. The Goblin tapped his foot and the Unicorn began to whistle.

"That's one vote for the Humans!" said the Goblin. "Now, who votes for the Unicorns?"

The Unicorn couldn't manage to raise his hoof above his head, so he waved his horn around vigorously.

"I don't see any votes for the Unicorns," said the Goblin. "Therefore the Goblins and the Humans are real creatures and the Unicorns are make-believe."

"That's not fair!" snorted the Unicorn. "I was voting with my horn!"

The Goblin's eyes grew wide.

"But you said only a minute ago that that horn wasn't even real!"

"But it IS REAL!" cried the Unicorn. "Take a look here, where it joins onto my head!"

"If it is real," growled the Goblin, "that means you're a Unicorn and Unicorns have just been voted as make-believe."

"Well, let's vote on horses then!" begged the troubled quadruped.

The Goblin rolled his eyes.

"If you were a horse, you wouldn't be talking, would you?"

"But if I didn't talk," whinnied the Unicorn, "you wouldn't be listening!"

"Listen, Unicorn," snapped the Goblin, "stop pretending to be a horse: horses are even more make-believe than Unicorns are. Horses live in the same realm as Human Beings, on a big ball that turns through space and more space and more and more and more space. Don't lower yourself to that level of fantasy!"

"Wait a minute, wait a minute, now!" I interrupted. "I remember now: we do, in fact, have horses on my planet Earth that CAN talk and DO have very beautiful horns that protrude from their foreheads!"

The Goblin leapt up and screamed:

"Horses can NOT talk! The Human is just saying that because he wants you to be on his side! Unicorns are a much 'realer' species than mere Humans are! Unicorns are as real as real can be — just like Goblins!"

I pushed the Goblin aside.

"Just listen to his voice, Mister Unicorn — I mean, MISTER HORSE. That Goblin is sounding more and more hoarse the more he shouts, so you're not the only one with a horse voice!"

The Unicorn held his head up high.

"Well, it seems to me that I am now worth two votes: one vote from Mister Goblin because he now says that Unicorns are just as real as Goblins; one vote from Mister Human, who says that I am in fact a very real horse from his aforementioned very real planet."

"But that's cheating!" shrieked the Goblin. "You can't be a horse AND a Unicorn at once!"

The Unicorn shrugged.

"It's not up to me who thinks who is what. It's up to the voter how he interprets what he sees!"

The Goblin clenched both fists.

"Well, all I see is a make-believe Unicorn, found only in fantasy stories and New Age bookshops!"

I had to hold the Goblin back.

"Okay, listen to me — this is all getting out of hand. Who cares if anyone is make-believe or real? We're all HERE, aren't we? Why don't we all just BELIEVE that EVERYONE is real and forget all about it?"

There was a long silence, then the Goblin said:

"If we all make-believe that everyone is real, that means we'd even be making-believe that the real ones were real, and if everybody were just make-believe, we'd be in REAL trouble!"

"Well, I think you're REALLY stupid!" I yelled.

The Goblin laughed.

"I'd rather be REALLY stupid than MAKE-BELIEVE AND STUPID like yourself!"

I threw my hands up.

"Okay, okay, I—give—up! — This whole story is just make-believe anyway!"

"What do you mean?" demanded the Goblin.

"This whole story is just fiction and I'm just making up the whole thing."

"A Dictator!" yelled the Unicorn.

"So!" said the Goblin. "This is all your make-believe Story, and now you're tired of it, so you're out of here and going back to your 'more space and more space and more and more and more space' world?"

I crossed my arms.

"Yes, that's correct and I think I've said MORE than enough!"

The pair began to dance around again, chanting "More space and more space and more and more and more space!" over and over. The Goblin winked at me and said:

"That's your story, son, and you stick to it!"

Rewind

"And they both lived happily ever after – in the afterlife", whispered Eric Springfield to himself. He turned the ignition key and reversed out of the cemetery car park, then continued backing along the entire length of Cemetery Road. He swung around a corner and continued reversing along Ocean Boulevard. The sun peeped over the horizon before him. He watched it rise into the cloudless sky, as incidents from the previous night flashed through his mind.

Melanie had seemed perfectly sane to begin with. In fact, Eric thought he may have even met the future Mrs Springfield. But when they stumbled through her front door, he froze when he saw a Policeman's Helmet handing on the coat-stand. Eric, though very drunk, bade a hasty retreat but Melanie managed to convince him that her marriage was over and her husband wouldn't be coming home. Just as Eric was beginning to unwind on the couch, Melanie spilt two glasses of red wine straight down his front. She helped him out of his clothes but then went and fetched a Police uniform for him to wear.

As he continued reversing along Ocean Boulevard, the sun was now shining over the city. He stubbed a cigarette butt in the ashtray. A smoke ring appeared from thin air and shrunk, as it disappeared into his mouth. The cigarette grew longer as he took a deep drag. More smoke rings materialised before him and one by one they followed the first one into Eric's mouth.

Melanie had been entranced when he marched around her lounge in the uniform. She insisted on putting a cigarette in his mouth and repeatedly tried to light it, but Eric had refused, as smoking had always disgusted him. He told her that she was under arrest and that a strip search was in order. He chased her around the house, both of them laughing hysterically whilst knocking furniture over. He followed her out the front door to the driveway. She jumped in her car and wailed "Come on! Let's go for a picnic. It's a full moon!"

Eric squinted in the morning sun, as he continued backing along Ocean Boulevard. When his cigarette reached its full length, he took the car's cigarette lighter from its socket and held it at the tip of his cigarette until it was no longer alight. He then placed the cigarette into its packet. Something didn't seem quite right to Eric this morning but he couldn't put his finger on what it was. Then he remembered that he had never before blown smoke rings let alone sucked them out of thin air, then he also remembered that he had never smoked a cigarette before in his life.

Melanie had driven Eric to the cemetery. After a short session of kissing and groping in the car, she had jumped out and ran laughing through the gates. Eric gave chase. She dodged around some trees and a few tombstones, then he caught her by the arm and they collapsed in a heap amongst some freshly cut flowers.

As Eric climbed on top of her, she began to groan in a harrowing way that alarmed him. She cried out "Peter, I knew you'd come back to me!" Eric opened his eyes to see a gravestone inches from his face. REST IN PEACE, PETER ALFRED COYLE. DIED WHILST SERVING THE PUBLIC IN A JOB HE LOVED.

Eric pressed the cigarette lighter into its socket, as he backed around a corner and came to a swift halt in a Police Station car park. A Sergeant emerged from another car and made his was over to Eric.

"Mister Eric Springfield! Nice of you to drop in. We've been waiting twelve months to talk with you in connection with the murder of Sergeant Peter Coyle. May I ask how you've come to be driving his old car? It's strange too, how you chose this parking space. It used to be reserved for Sergeant Coyle, once upon a time."

A Change of Heart

Rahni switched off the light and snuggled in beside Peter.

"Pete, Darling, Mummy and Daddy think the world of you! We had a good long talk after dinner and, though they don't speak a word of English, they said they could tell you were a wonderful man by your face and your body language, and guess what?"

"What?"

"Daddy said he'd fly us both to Pakistan for a traditional wedding. Isn't that wonderful?!"

"That's brilliant, Rahni, but I thought them being so posh'n'all, they wouldn't want their daughter to marry a cleaner."

"Well, I have to explain about that Pete."

"Explain what?"

"Well, I was trying to explain to them that you clean operating theatres at the hospital."

"Yeah? – And?"

"Well, I was trying to explain to them what a hygiene technician was, but I couldn't translate it very well into Hindi and – and they got the idea that you were actually a surgeon."

"A surgeon – shit – I was wondering why they suddenly took a shine to me!"

"Oh Pete, I tried to tell them the truth, but – but they got so excited – it's the first time they've ever been eager to see me married – they were so proud of me and I didn't want to spoil it!"

"Oh well, I suppose I could just ponce about with some medical books when we get there."

"But there's another problem."

"Another problem? What?"

"Well, they – they wanted to see you working at the hospital before they flew home."

"What? See me mopping a bloody floor?!"

"Pete, Darling, I told them you were doing a heart transplant tomorrow evening, because I know they were flying out tomorrow afternoon – but their flight was delayed 24 hours."

"Oh, shit, Rahni, what'll I do now?"

"Pete, can't you just pretend for five minutes at work that you're a surgeon for their little visit? Then they'd go back to Pakistan and tell all the relatives – they'd all be so proud of us!"

Peter lay awake staring at the ceiling for half the night, wondering why life had to be so complicated. It cost him a fortnight's wages to pay his colleagues to do the deed. They were all to assemble in theatre six – the least used theatre in the hospital – all dressed up in theatre greens, gloves and masks to stage a mock operation on a freshly retrieved corpse from the morgue (the corpse costing £30 for 15 minutes, going straight into Reg Harrelson's pocket, the creepy little bastard). Rahni's parents would arrive, peek through the small window in the door, see their high achieving future son-in-law in action, then be whisked off by Rahni sight seeing around London. Then, with operation "OPERATION" completed, all the cleaners could return to their mopping.

Peter waited in the car park, chain smoking. As arranged, Rahni drove in with her parents at two minutes past seven. Peter darted to the lift, went up to the fourth floor, threw on a gown, mask and gloves, then entered theatre six. He was impressed by the scene that awaited him.

"Well done, guys, you all look great. You've even splashed blood on your gowns for extra effect! Stand aside now lads, let the Head Surgeon through!"

But, as Peter elbowed his way through, a gruesome sight befell him. The corpse's chest had been opened wide with tubes and clamps stuck everywhere. The heart, having been removed, was placed neatly beside the body.

"Jesus Christ, guys, you didn't have to mutilate the poor sod – we could have just pretended – what if the relatives want to view it? -Who's gonna stitch it all up again? Bloody hell, don't you have any respect for the dead?"

But, as Peter's eyes met theirs, he had an even bigger shock. For they weren't his friends at all – but real surgeons.

"Shit, I'm in theatre six on the fourth floor – I should be in theatre six down on the fifth!"

"It's alright, Pete," said the real head surgeon, "you've come to the right place, come over here and take a look at the patient's face."

Peter nearly fainted on the spot.

"Holy shit – it's me!" he gasped. "What the hell is happening here?"

"It's a heart transplant, Peter. We're taking the real heart from Peter the Cleaner and we're going to pop it inside you now to create Peter the real live respectable heart surgeon, get it?"

The theatre workers then advanced on him, brandishing scalpels and other strange implements. Peter awoke clutching at his chest.

"Pete, darling, are you alright – you were screaming in your sleep!"

"I've had a change of heart Rahni. 'Pete the cleaner' and 'Rahni the counter assistant' are getting married here in London in a Registry Office. There will be a celebration here at the flat afterwards with sausage rolls and club sandwiches on the menu. All your relatives are invited but, if they don't turn up, I won't be getting cut up about it."

The Ernest Hemingway Trophy

We like to call this hallway 'Hemingway's Ark'. All of these wonderful beasts have been bought together here from all around the world – stuffed, mounted and preserved for everyone to enjoy!

Wow – it really is like an ark – only its so, so quiet – dead quiet – and everything's so still – so dead still!

Mister Hemingway shot one or more of every species mounted along this wall. All these exhibits have been arranged in chronological order beginning with the first beast the boy Hemingway ever shot right through to his magnificent African safari trophies. Don't touch please, there's a good lad! The name Hemingway translates roughly into Chinese as 'The Hunter of Wolves', something the writer was immensely proud of. The best examples of his passion for hunting and his genius for story telling can be found in his novel 'The Green Hills of Africa' and, of course, his two classic short stories 'The Snows of Kilimanjaro' and 'The Short Happy Life of Francis Macomber'. We begin the Ernest Hemingway Story with the very first thing the boy Hemingway ever shot.

A weasel?

That's right lad! Hemingway shot this specimen soon after his twelfth birthday. His father had given him a twenty-gauge shotgun as a birthday present – it was also at this point of his life that he began to write short stories. This tiny specimen marks the beginning of two equally successful careers in hunting and story telling. Moving along to the right, we have a squirrel and a deer – two fine mementoes from an adventurous boyhood shot by Ernest at the age of fifteen and seventeen respectively.

Excuse me, but wasn't Mister Hemingway quoted as saying that he had a 'gift for killing' and that he 'loved to kill animals'?

Young man there are always armies of 'wanna bees' who quote successful people out of context just to get their own names into newspapers. Mister Hemingway *did* have compassion for animals: he had no less than fifteen pet cats, each of which the writer himself named according to their personalities. He also regarded elephants as being far too noble a creature for humans to shoot.

But, if he loved cats and noble beasts so much, why is there a big lion's head on the wall?

Young man, some things Mister Hemingway regarded as 'huntable' and other things he regarded as not 'huntable' - every man has to draw the line somewhere. Mister Hemingway shot this magnificent trophy at the age of thirty-two, along with the leopard and jaguar also shot during his thirty-second year. Here, we see how the young enthusiast evolved into the big game hunter the world came to love and admire. Any serious hunter would give his eye-tooth for a collection like this! Moving along, to the right we have the Nobel Prize awarded to Ernest at the age of fifty-five. By this stage of his life, he had enchanted the entire world with his extraordinary fiction and his own gallant life-style. He was widely regarded as the greatest writer and adventurer of the Twentieth Century. He once said that if he couldn't hunt, his life would not be worth living.

What's this last specimen on the very end here? It's dated the second of July 1961. Is this the last thing he ever shot? It's got a white beard? Is it Noah himself?

New Rage 1

Just imagine right? One of those enamelled yin and yang badges. You know the ones - with the two little tadpoles in it? One's black with a white-eye and the other's white with a black eye. Now just imagine a pair of very sharp-ended tweezers wheedling their way beneath the enamel, pinching onto the black tadpole's tail and tearing it right out of the symbol. All that's left is a white circle with a little black dot and watch now as that little black dot starts dissolving like a black aspirin on your tongue, turning the whole symbol a murky grey. Well that's what Donna did to me – *she stole my fucking yang!*

    I live at the very top of the Morton Flats on the twenty-second floor. There are also twenty-two vertebrae in the human spine, incredible isn't it? The Lord Buddha pointed out that to live was to suffer. This building is filled with human suffering. On the first floor we have Sweaty Betty the old prostitute who somehow manages to get the Concierge to clean her landing whenever it's her turn. On the fourth floor we have Stevie D who feeds his pet python on the things he finds running around the place. He is also the proud owner of the largest selection of snuff movies on the Estate. On the seventh floor we have Cassandra who had a drug overdose two years ago and lost ninety five percent of her eyesight.

    Someone asked the Buddha once why he was laughing as he walked up a steep hill "Because I shall soon be walking down hill" was his reply.

    Cassandra now has a career, going round to all the schools with her dog lecturing on the dangers of drugs. She is the only career person in the building.

    On the fifteenth floor we have Ralf and Sarah Meadows, who won thirteen hundred pounds on the lottery.

    Someone asked the Buddha once why he was crying as he walked downhill.

    Ralf had old gambling debts out-standing from way back.

Next thing two heavies arrive at his door, beat the living shit out of him and take all the winnings.

Anyway I am getting off the path here, lets just say that every other bastard I didn't mention is a junky or a shrivelled up little television addict who sees the outside world through the little fish eye lens mounted in their front door.

The Buddha pointed out that the lotus flower takes root in mud and rises up through the murkiest of waters.

Years ago Donna bought me a book about Kundalini. Kundalini is the spiritual process that takes place when the yogi sees through the material world and down through his past lives to the Atman – the very essence of existence, where all is revealed and everything and nothing is known. Mystic energies then focus at the base of the spine, a serpent uncoils and rises up through the chakras to the nape of the neck up to the crown of the head and then right over the forehead and stops at the space between the eyes. This is when the third eye is opened. Kudalini can only begin when the yogi's yin and yang are in perfect harmony.

Everyone in this building is trapped in the cycle of birth and rebirth. Nothing new ever happens here. Even jumping off your balcony is old hat. Donna and I were heavily into each other, we knew the Kama Sutra back to front. We were also heavily into grass. Donna had to be tied up to get turned on. She particularly liked fine ropes that she could later modify into bracelets for her wrists and ankles. She'd always disappear for a day or two after sex and go hitching around busking or reading Tarot cards. She was the typical free spirited Sagittarian. She told me that she liked to fondle her bracelets whilst on the road because it made her feel close to me. She said they were charged with my yang.

I didn't mind tying her up: I'd do anything to give her pleasure. But when she asked me to hit her it was against my second precept. We had a big argument and she stormed out and didn't return for twenty-six days. There was no letter or postcard – nothing. I was sick with worry and loneliness. Meditation was the only thing that kept me sane. I would sit in the lotus position by my window and gaze out over the city and to the distant hills wondering where she was. The trouble is, my flat is so close to the lift that I could hear it every time it started to rise.

It always starts off with three kinds of guitar notes which must be the cables pulling tight. Then comes the slow train, bowling alley drum roll, that echoes right through me as the lift moves up through the shaft. Every time that fucking thing sparks up I jump out of my skin – sit bolt upright, every sinew and tendon in my body pulling tight. My heartbeat races as I urge the lift to rise higher and higher.

Day followed day but she didn't show. Sometimes the lift rose all the way up to my level causing my scalp to break out in sweat. The doors would swish open and my stupid fucking next-door neighbour would saunter out. That's when I felt like jumping off the balcony. That's when I began to sample my stores to calm me down a bit.

I store produce for some clients a few floors down. The cops busted them three times in a row and got nothing: it is a good little system. I have no criminal record and the boys bring the produce up the stairs so they're not caught on C.C.T.V in the lift and for my services they drop off incense and fruit as I no longer venture into the material world.

When Donna arrived on that twenty-sixth day I broke down in tears and fell at her feet. There was no great explanation as to where she'd been and as my elation wore off I got I got angrier and angrier. It was the way she just kept shrugging to every question that fucked me off. I got the feeling that the only reason she came back was because her bracelets had lost their yang charge. When I told her that I'd developed the ability to see down through all the floors like glass and that all the other people in the building were my past lives she just laughed like a witch. Then she said that my spiritual journey was nothing but an ego trip! I blacked out completely. Imagine the black tadpole trying to suffocate the white one. Imagine its tail transforming into that of a scorpion. Imagine the scorpion tail driving straight into the whiteness. All I can remember is unbuckling my belt and feeling the end snake around my waist, jolting through the belt loops

– unleashing and then blackness.

    I opened one eye in the middle of the loneliest, darkest night of my life. But I could feel her there in my arms, warm. At least I hadn't killed her. When I awoke in the morning she was gone and so was my belt.

    I don't sleep anymore. I have to be aware at all times. Awareness is the most important thing in spiritual life. If I was to sleep now she might arrive at my door and disappear again for another two hundred and seventy three days. Sometimes I can see her in my mind's eye, alone in a room, holding my yang by the buckle, snaking it up around her leg, up her back and over her shoulder, around her neck and across her lips, down between her breasts around her waist, beneath her buttocks and up between her legs.

    The tabs have yin and yang symbols on them. I place another one on my tongue. I savour its bitterness as it slowly dissolves turning my world murky grey.

New Rage (Part 2)

Men with small cocks design high rise buildings. Jason lived at the top of a giant cock. There were seven high risers in the housing scheme. The Morton Tower stood a clear two stories higher than all the others. This gave Jason an immense sense of satisfaction.

I was a new woman. Reborn from Mother Earth herself! I'd spent the best part of nine months within Mother Nature's womb, protesting underground, protecting her from a rash of small membered men in bulldozers intent on carving her up with a massive phallic highway. It's only when you're deep down within her, that you can feel her heartbeat, see her root systems feel the life force in her walls.

Jason had no understanding of the cycle of life. The only stuff he ever recycled were his daft Buddhist sayings. He used to say, "If a tree falls down in the middle of a forest and no one's there to hear it, does it make a sound?" Jason had never been out of the city or really looked at a tree. I remember he nearly jumped out of his body when he found a tiny spider in the bath. I said to him once, I said, "If a tree grows in the middle of a city and everyone's too occupied to look at it, is it actually there?" He gave me one of his daft cosmic looks so I whacked him one, straight across the face "That, my Grasshopper, was the sound of *one hand slapping!*" that's what Masters do to monks in Zen monasteries to shock them into enlightenment, but I think I just bruised his male ego!

When Jason and I used to fuck five times a day, this whole housing scheme used to hear about it, then when the drugs took over and Jason couldn't get wood, an eerie silence descended over the concrete jungle.

Don't get me wrong, I love cock just as much as anyone and Jason had the greatest prick in the world. But 'cock' needs to know its place. When it gets too big for its balls it needs to come back down to earth, otherwise it destroys everything in its path, whilst destroying itself.

And when I say "cock" I don't just mean "penis", "cock" is a state of mind. Take Margaret Thatcher, she has more balls than any other Premier in history and what is she doing? She's shagging the single mothers, shafting the miners, fucking this country *right up!* It's because of *her* that I have to go underground to save Mother Earth from total destruction and Jason's stuck up there in the clouds, zenning out the world below that has no place for him.

The candle used to throw animated shadows all around the walls of my earth womb. When you're underground, day in day out and all alone, the mind becomes extremely perceptive. Once, I was laying naked on my back, I rested Jason's belt down the length of my body. All of a sudden I saw that the belt was a replica of the highway they were trying to build above me – running through the countryside. I was seeing into the future. Jason had punched extra holes into his belt because he was grossly underweight. From my angle all those little holes looked just like the lines painted down the centre of a road. I knew there and then that I must abort my protest. I held the belt up in front of the candle, a wobbling vertical shadow appeared upon the wall. It looked just like the Morton Flats and there was even a line of little windows where the candlelight shone through the holes. I focussed on that little top window, I focused with all my being.

The closer I bought the belt to the candle, the bigger the window became. There was nothing but white light in there until I saw grey smoke emanating from it. The belt had caught alight! My earth womb quickly turned grey. I started to choke and I blacked out. The Police dragged me out and then went down to check if anybody else was down there. They handed me the remains of the belt which was nothing much more than the buckle. It had lost all its yang. I knew then that I had to go back to Jason.

The clitoris has forty two percent more nerve endings than the penis. The average female orgasm lasts two and a half times longer than that of the male. Female hemp is two and a half times more potent than male hemp. Maurice, the truck driver, I hitched a lift with, seemed well impressed with this information and drove me all the way up to Morton Road.

    I lit a spliff and gazed upwards. Dead straight lines all pointed to Jason's flat. It had been drizzling and the high rise was a murky tombstone colour. I got out my chalk and drew three wiccan signs on the footpath by the entrance. The light in the lift was smashed. I pushed the 22 button, someone had drawn a yin and yang sign on it with a marker pen. I took a long toke on my spliff and up I went, shooting through the eye of the giant cement cock. All the different floors flickered past, they just went on and on and for a while there I thought I was being ejaculated all the way up to heaven!

Guinea Pigs

Traffic in the High Street was held up for two and a half-hours yesterday afternoon, due to a protest march by an estimated three and a half thousand local guinea pigs. The organiser of the march, known only as Dumpy, stated that guinea pigs the world over were sick and tired of being stereotyped as mere entities of experimentation.

"Calling someone a 'guinea pig' when they are being subjected to new and potentially dangerous situations," said Dumpy, "only sustains the belief that we are nothing more than vermin, useful only for laboratory experimentation and detracts from our other qualities such as intelligence, sensitivity and cuteness."

When asked if any legal action would be taken against the guinea pigs for obstructing the traffic, Local Police Sergeant Brian Hill replied that "The matter was still being looked into – the guinea pig protest being the first ever case of its kind."

Jesus versus Jesus

Last Easter, our Sunday school teacher, Mrs Wright, bought a big slab of clay in and cut it up into equal cubes. Everyone got a cube each and we all had to make a Jesus to go on the wooden cross we'd made the week before. She said whoever made the best Jesus would win the big chocolate Easter egg on her table. We all got to work and my Jesus was looking really cool – tons better than everyone else's.

Danny's Jesus didn't even have a beard; Geoff's Jesus had football shorts on! Nicole's Jesus looked like a ginger bread man and Rodney's Jesus looked like a scarecrow.

Anyway, I had to go to the toilet and when I got back, my Jesus had a big pointy nose squashed onto his face and someone had given him pointy ears like Mister Spock. Sally asked me why I was going bright red and then she started giggling. I would have told Mrs Wright straight away but she was somewhere outside putting Easter decorations up. When she came back, I was about to tell her what had happened but then I had a better idea. During our lunch break, I snuck back into the classroom and did some alterations on five of the other Jesus's – some of them I didn't have to worry about – they were silly enough the way they were. I deliberately left Sally's Jesus alone and damaged my own to throw everyone's suspicion onto her.

When everyone came back in from lunch, Mrs Wright was out again doing the decorations. Julie yelled out "Oh, look, my Jesus has glasses." When everyone started complaining, I joined in for extra effect. Everyone blamed Sally and started messing with her Jesus. She tried to run off with him but he slipped off his cross and plopped onto the floor, so I jumped on him. Then Sally whacked me with the empty cross – so I went and got my cross and we had a sword fight with them. Then everyone did the same, so it looked like a scene out of Peter Pan. When Mrs Wright came back, there were squashed Jesus' everywhere. Needless to say, nobody won the Easter egg. We had to peel all the squashed Jesus' up and roll them all up into one big round ball. Mrs Wright yelled at us all for being so petty and childish. I had never seen her so angry – and to top it off, she went and got hit in the eye that night at the Catholic – Protestant clash at Fordhan Street.

The War To End All Wars

(Translated from Zertos)

Gentlemen, this will be the war to end all wars. Mankind has never known such sophisticated weaponry. Every conflict that has gone before has amounted to this day. Now, we must fight to the bitter end to rid the world of evil forever. So let's all pick up our clubs and spears and get out there and fight.

Hounded

When Dodi and Diana came through the rotating doors, the Paparazzi dashed to their cars and motorcycles. The Mercedes Benz sped off, with the press hot on their heels, blasting their horns through the cool night air.

Prince William, in his bright red hunting coat, sat proudly on his stallion. When the horn sounded, the horses and the hounds sprang into action. William held tightly onto the reins, as they charged across the field.

Trying to outfox the Paparazzi, the Mercedes Benz took an unexpected route through some side streets. By the time it reached the tunnel, only a few of the press were still on the trail.

The fox darted into a rabbit warren only to discover that it was too narrow even for her slender body.

The Mercedes hit a pylon inside the tunnel and spun out of control.

The pack of reporters surrounded the dying woman, too busy flashing their cameras to offer any assistance.

By the time the corpse was retrieved from the hounds it was barely recognisable. The Hunt Master smeared blood on Prince William's face. William smiled proudly for a photographer.

Flash! Flash! Flash! Flash!

Prince William walked solemnly behind the coffin as it moved through the crowded streets. How could human beings do such a thing to one so beautiful?

Harold Wolfrey's Last Christmas

It had been exactly four years since Harold Wolfrey had taken the embroidered tablecloth out from the linen drawer and it had been exactly four years since Harold's family had come together for Christmas. With reverence he carried the tablecloth over to the dining room table and spread it out, giving it a little tug here and there so that it was perfectly centred. Memories of the family's last Christmas together came flooding back to him. There had been lots of presents, lots of food and laughter, and lots of drinking and arguing.

He sat down at the table and took a folded red paper hat out of his pocket, unfolded it, and placed it on his head. He then removed three videophones from his coat pocket and placed them on the table before him. One by one he turned each phone on and stood them up in a semi-circular formation so that everyone could see everyone else. On the telephone screen to Harold's left appeared his twenty four-year-old daughter Tarquin who was now living in Brisbane, Australia.

She yelled excitedly "Merry Christmas Daddy! How's London?" Then when Tarquin's mothers face materialised to her left she screamed "Merry Christmas Mum, is it snowing in Washington D.C?"

Gloria Wolfrey had left Harold for a younger man three years ago "I don't want to talk about snow, Tarquin, I want to see my new Grandson!" Tarquin proudly held up a healthy gurgling baby.

"Harold!" whined Gloria, "Bring Tarquin's phone closer to mine so I can get a good look at my grandson!"

Harold bought the two phones together, then danced them around each other. "Oh, Tarquin Darling, he's beautiful", cried Gloria.

A tear rolled off Harold's cheek onto the tablecloth. "It's been far too long since we had a traditional Christmas get together" he blubbered. He placed the two phones back in their places. Tarquin's face had dropped "Where's Shane? Why is his screen blank?" Harold shook his head in exasperation. "He's probably out at a night-club; he never was very family orientated"

"Oh *Harold*!" scolded Gloria "For goodness sake, stop bringing everybody down!"

Tarquin offered, "His phone network might be overloaded in Hong Kong at this time of year."

"That's right Darling" assured her mother.

Harold rolled his eyes "Maybe he can't get a good reception on the dance floor"

"Right Harold! Any more of that and I'm switching off" said Gloria "And I will too!" added her daughter. Harlold grumbled under his breathe "He could have made the effort for Christmas"

Harold left the table to pour himself a very large scotch while the women chatted about the baby. Harold returned all excited "I know, lets all have a sing along like we did in the good old days!" He picked up the two phones and stood them on the piano. Harold belted out Jingle Bells on the piano whilst he and the two women sang along like robots "Its just not the same without Shane" said Tarquin "I hope he's alright wherever he is!"

Harold carried the two mobiles back to the table. It was time to say farewell. After the two women hung up, Harold sat there looking at the three mobiles. They looked like tombstones. He wiped tears away with the edge of the tablecloth. The flat was dead silent.

The sound of the doorbell made him jump an inch off his seat "Surely not Carol singers at this time of night?" He crept over to the front door and peered up at the C.C.T.V screen. Shane was standing there, outside, with his arm around another man. Shane pushed the button again, Harold jolted then silently lowered himself onto the floor, relieved that he had pulled the curtains across earlier.

"Hello Dad!" came Shane's voice "Are you there dad? Brendan and I are on our way to Belfast for my second exhibition. This was meant to be a surprise but our plane was delayed and we'll have to rush back for the connecting flight." Harold was studying the design on the carpet, there were three different colours, he'd never looked at it so closely. "I sold five paintings last month, dad and things are looking up, and guess what? I'm in love! I've bought Brendan along with me, I'm sorry he's not a girl but he can't help it! I don't know if you can hear me dad but I've also bought along a painting for you. It's of a tree with a branch nailed back on." Shane tried to slide the painting under the door causing Harold to recoil. The opening was too narrow so he leant it against the front door. "Bye Dad – Merry Christmas!" "Merry Christmas, Mr Wolfrey!" called Brendan. Harold sat there studying every little tuft of the carpet for another hour before making his way off to bed. The following morning he opened the front door but the painting had vanished. "Probably those yobs from upstairs" he grumbled.

Seeds

Dougie was seven years old when he went to live with his Uncle Callum and Auntie Heather on the croft in the Highlands. His uncle yelled at the Clydesdale horse as he guided it across the fertile earth. Dougie walked along behind the big rake throwing handfuls of seeds from a big hessian bag that was slung over his shoulder. Coming from the Gorbals in Glasgow, Dougie couldn't believe that such wee dead things could grow all the way up to his own height.

The next morning he ran excitedly out to the field but there were no crops to be seen. He was convinced that the previous days graft had been a waste of time. Uncle Callum explained to him that that the seeds were part of a cycle that was so big and slow that it would be a few weeks before the green shoots appeared.

One dreich day that same season, Dougie found his father's war medals in his Uncle's bottom drawer. He couldn't remember his Father, he was three when he had fallen in action. Uncle Callum had buried the medals deep beneath a pile of old business papers. Wide eyed, Dougie held them up by their satin ribbons and spun them with his index finger. This was as close to his father that he could ever be.

Eleven seasons later Dougie had grown to over six feet tall and could single-handedly scythe and bind a paddock of wheat in a day. On Market day, they drove the truck fully laden with produce to Glasgow. Bagpipes and drums were blazing away in St. Enoches Square. There were Military men with rows of medals and ribbons pinned to their chests. In the midday sunshine, row upon row of young soldiers stood proud and erect. A sign said "Your Country Needs You Now! Sign On Today!"

"I'm signin' on the noo, Callum!" said Dougie.

"Ya cannae be serious, Dougie. Ah cannae run the croft without ye lad! And what about your new wife? She'll be givin' birth in April!"

"But its somethin' I feel deep down inside and anyway, they say we'll be back before sowing season".

Strawberry Wine

Becky suffers from low blood pressure. She sleeps all day long for rejuvenation. I always check the rosiness of her cheeks to be sure that she is ready to rise. As her eyelids lift I am faced with the only chink of blue sky I ever have to see. She always has a sore throat – she hasn't spoken in years – but her murmurings and slanting facial expressions always speak volumes. I spend so much time watching her sleep it feels a little crowded when her consciousness re-enters the room. As I raise her to her feet her long red hair falls perfectly into place, I have been brushing it out across the pillows for the past hour.

I always have a bowl of luscious strawberries prepared for her "Eat them up, Darling" I tell her "They're from our own garden – they'll give you strength for our nightly stroll." I lead her out through the back door and we drift along the overgrown path. The cold night air awakens her (as much as she can be awakened). She frowns at me as if to say "Why am I wearing my summer dress on such a cold and windy night?" I envelope her in the protective folds of my dressing gown. The path forms a rectangle within the high walls of the garden. Everything is overgrown. The gardener left us three years ago. He had been a meticulous pruner and sculpted fantastic animal shapes from the hedges. Even now, sometimes those beasts can re-appear if the moonlight catches them at the right angle. Though we no longer have a vegetable patch, this household still prides itself on self-sustainable means.

The rear garden wall is completely covered with vines. Becky and I always stop beside the frozen fountain. I like to watch her lily-white feet as she steps between the strawberry plants, so very close to where the gardener now lays. With frosted breath I whisper "Do you remember this place Darling?" Shaking from the cold she returns to the folds of my gown like a little lost bird.

I turn her white face up to the moonlight and the whole starry sky fills her pupils. "You hurt me deeply Rebecca, you hurt me very

very deeply" my shadow eclipses her face as I steal a kiss from her cruel lips. I guide her back to the house, wash her feet and stand her by the bed. I gently draw her hair behind her shoulder and trace my finger down the length of her neck. The sight of blue veins through translucent flesh causes me to salivate uncontrollably. Her head falls back a little and she smiles at me the very same way she smiled at him that day. I drive my fangs in with lightning speed, her body tightens and then contorts like a skewered snake but she doesn't have much strength. Her strawberry wine wells up at the top of my gums then gushes to the back of my throat. A delicious combination of nausea and euphoria overwhelms me. Her legs collapse beneath her and I gracefully lower her onto the bed whilst continuing to feed from her throat. I place a finger over her wrist to feel her dancing pulse, I have to be careful not to over indulge.

Gloating and bloated I manoeuvre myself away from the bed and stumble out to the garden. I crouch down by the fountain with my head in my hands and I can see through my minds eye with crystal clarity, the gardener standing on this very spot on that fateful day. I see sunlight shining through Becky's hair. I see him hand her that strawberry. I see the outline of her body through that summer dress. I see her twirling that strawberry in the fountain, then placing it between her teeth. I can see him stroking her wavy hair and moving in very close to her and taking a bite from the strawberry. The sickly tang of strawberry juice accosts my own lips. I see myself kill him over and over again.

When I hear the first bird sing I stand and stretch then urinate all over the strawberry plants. Its important to return the nitrates to the soil, this household prides itself on self-sufficiency. I race back to the house before the garden is drowned in sunlight.

If Only –

If only you could have lived when those around you
Were falling – your mother and I had such love for you.
If only you'd seen through all the hype to confound you;
From childhood and right through your teenage years too.
If only you'd known of the horrors that lay waiting, where reality's
Bayonet stabs the mistiest eyes.
If only you'd time for questioning and debating
Fought the real World War against deception and lies.

If only you had not made other men your masters;
If only you didn't have to carry my name;
If only when you'd felt a hero or a coward
You'd treated those two impostors just the same;
If only you could have been more outspoken,
Not believing the words of each Government fool;
If only you could see now the promises broken,
You might not have been such a willing tool.

If only politics could dawn with a new beginning,
Not staking young lives at pitch and toss –
They repeatedly tell us our Country is winning!
The dead don't reply with their views on their loss.
If only somehow you could have known what to do
But in war, who's to say what is right, what is wrong?
Were God, King and Country out there to protect you,
Or mere heirlooms to sacrifice your life upon?

*If only you could have walked away with your virtue
Or grown up a King – for guns they never will touch.
If only God in his mercy could've spared you;
If only he'd seen that so many loved you so much;
If only he could have granted us another full minute –
How could he let so many soldiers die so young?
Yours would have been the Earth and all that's in it:
You would have been a man – my lost fallen son.*

Roundabout

There I was putt-putting along, out in the middle of nowhere in me old Austin A40, when all of a sudden I come to this roundabout. You know how it is when you're old, your concentration wanders off sometimes. Well, by the time that Give Way sign registered in me brain, I was half way across that god-damned roundabout. Then I hear this god almighty skid and this flash o' red streak past, missin' me by inches. He must 'a been doin' a good ninety miles an hour 'cos it took him ages to come to a standstill. Blue smoke was everywhere: he must 'ave left half his tyres on that bitumen.

Next thing he's spinnin' his tyres in reverse, headin' straight back towards me. At first, I thought he was comin' back to see if I was all right, but how wrong was I? This young fella leaps out of the M.G. wavin' his arms around and swearin' at me, "Outta the car, ya old bastard, I'm gonna break ya fuckin' neck. Well, don't just sit there. Get out!" Then his girlfriend tries to get in on the act, "Go on Nick, hit 'im, he could of killed us!" Nick whips open my door and drags me out onto the road. "Get up so I can knock you down again, Baldy. Come on, old boy!" The funny thing was, as I'm cowerin', there on the road, his number plate leaps out at me KOM 327 – that's my old number plate from *years* ago – 'n that car – the red M.G. – that's *my* old car!

"Get up now, arsehole, you're just gonna make it worse for yourself!" he says.

But somehow I know he's gonna try 'n' kick me in the head, so I dive outta the way just in time to see his boot swish past me left ear.

"Jesus Christ!" yells Nick. "Not bad reflexes for a Senior Citizen, eh, Sandra?"

I know that girl: it's Sandra Rushton — my first ever girlfriend — she ended up emptying my bank account and leaving me for my best friend, but she hasn't aged a day in forty years!? And then it hits me that I know this whole scene from my distant past because I *am* or I *was* that young man!

Ooof! Something spikes me right in the middle of the back and I know damned well it's the point of Sandra's shoe.

God damn the pain, then me whole body goes to pins and needles and the lad spits on me 'n' hisses: "Hope you fuckin' rot out 'ere, old boy!" The two of them laugh like hyenas as they go back to the sports car.

Tears fill me eyes as I watch it disappear into the horizon. But I don't feel anger, 'cos I know damned well where he is heading and what comes around *does* go around in a roundabout sort of way.

The Last Assignment

It had rained so much that Friday afternoon, Vinnie and me were starting to think she wouldn't show. It wasn't how I'd been imagining it for the last three days. She arrived eight minutes late in a blue raincoat. When she pulled the hood back little drops of rain were dripping from her hair down her forehead. She had a bit of mascara on. Vinnie held onto the assignment. He was my best mate and had helped with the haggling.

Rule number one stated that the snog would go for ninety-five seconds. Rule number two stated that Vinnie had to wait over by the seesaw and time it. Rule three – I could put my hands on her hips but they were not to move from there. Rule four – neither Vinnie or myself could ever mention the event to anyone else for the rest of our lives.

As if I wouldn't tell anyone else! Leonie McCloy was the hottest chick in Bruthan, if not the whole of East Gippsland. I was a pure dag – a nobody – thirteen months her junior who was just lucky enough to live two doors away. So what if her Barnsdale boyfriend knocked the shit out of me? A busted up face would be tangible evidence that a bloke who drives an XU1 Torana had a good reason to beat up a Malvern Star rider with a pudding-bowl haircut.

The kiss started off all right. I mean I'd snogged Raelene Holden at her brother's sixteenth and that was nice and I'd had my hand up Tania Orchards jumper on two occasions and that was grouse and this kiss was grouse too. To start off with, her lips were open just enough for me to get my tongue in so that I could just touch the tip of hers. It would have been all right if it had gone on just like that.

But maybe thirty or forty seconds into the snog her mouth opened a bit more and her lips kind of got a lot softer and I kind of went in a lot deeper and she was doing these strange kind of flourishes with her tongue. The underside of hers was enticing the tip of mine, then swirling around it and then enticing it again and I knew then that tongues were *made* to do this. I thought we could just do this forever and ever and always be happy.

Once, Vinnie and me had been swimming at the Bruthan Baths for about an hour. When we got out Vinnie opened a bag of Salt and Vinegar crisps. I was starvin' hungry and had no money so I asked him for some and he just handed me one little half-soggy crisp. There's something about eating salt and vinegar crisps after swimming in a chlorinated pool that makes them taste a thousand times better. Anyway, Vinnie, the prick, wouldn't give me any more, just danced around on the grass and ate the whole fucking pack. He knew that by just giving me one I'd get the taste for them and so he enjoyed them a lot more, knowin' I was drooling – he was a bastard like that. Leonie was doing the same thing with her tongue.

Anyway, at about the seventy second mark her lips weren't that soft anymore and her tongue just stayed still like a piece of rubber and I started to think about that face on the blow up doll that Vinnie and me found in the old caravan. Vinnie yelled out "O.K. that's ninety five seconds!" As we drew away I caught sight of her eyes and that's what kind of scared me. It was as if nothin' had even happened between us. She had really fucked with my head.

It would have been all right if she'd just been cold the whole time and it would have been all right if she'd been hot the whole time. But the way she just froze over did something to me. And the way she just picked up the fag she'd left burning for ninety five seconds and the way she picked up my homework assignment flicked through the pages to check it was all there and walked off without saying anything.

Vinnie bolted over to me all excited, lit two fags and handed me one. "Well, Trev? How'd it go? Did ya get a hard on?" I took a long drag and slowly exhaled the smoke downwards. There were a few slugs on the footpath. I wondered how they'd go about killing each other. "Well, come on, tell me, mate, was it fucking grouse or what?"

"Yeah, shit hot," I said "Let's get the football out. We haven't had a kick for ages."

The Three Way Split

As always Belief and Disbelief were at each other throats. Disbelief was yelling things like "I *don't believe* a word you're saying!" and Belief was screeching things like "I *believe* you're mistaken there!"

    Just then the two jumped back in shock "Ha! Ha! Look who's coming, it's God himself!" laughed Belief. "Now we'll see who's telling the truth! Hello God, how are you on this wonderful evening?" God shook his head slowly, "I'm as lonely as ever my friends. I could count on one hand the number of people who come to me and you two divide everyone else evenly between yourselves."

It Never Did Me Any Harm

"*Perkins!*"

"Y-y-yes, Miss Morrison."

"Come up here to the blackboard, young man … Hurry up, Perkins, we haven't all day! Now, Mister Perkins, what have you got in your mouth?"

"N-n-nothin', Miss."

"Open your mouth, Perkins … wider … wider … WIDER! Oh, Mr Perkins, we *do* seem to have a large round sweet lodged in the corner of our mouth, don't we? Did we forget that we'd put it in there earlier, did we? Now, I'm going to give you something, young man, that will improve your memory for the rest of your life!"

"M-miss, I won't do it again — I promise I won't!"

"Mister Perkins, repeat to the class what I stipulated only yesterday regarding the consumption of sweets in the classroom."

"Y-you said, Miss…"

"Speak up, Perkins, so we can ALL hear you!"

"You said that if anybody was caught eating sweets in class … they'd be caned, Miss."

"How many strokes, Perkins? Can you remember that as well?"

"S-six, Miss."

"Very good, we are all very impressed, Perkins! Now take that sweet out of your mouth and put it in the bin, there's a good chap. Now bend over and touch your toes. All the way down, Jonathan … that's right."

SWI-I-I-SH! — "*Ouch! — Ooowww!*"

"Stay down, Perkins, there's five more from where that came from!"

SWI-I-I-SH! — "*Ooow — ow-ow-ow!*"

"Oh, stop blubbering, Perkins, it's for your own good. You'll thank me for this one day!"

SW-I-I-I-I-SH! — "Oh, no more, please! No more, Miss!"

"When I was a pupil, Perkins, my teacher used to give me six of the best on a regular basis and it never did me any harm. Believe me, Perkins, it never did ME any harm. OK, Jonathan, that's your time up now."

"But I didn't orgasm!"

"Come on, Jonathan, you know the rules: a half-hour session is a half-hour session. If you want to go the full hour it'll be another fifty pounds."

"But I was just getting turned on!"

"Sorry, Jonathan, rules are rules."

"Oh, all right, all right. Can you book me in for the same time next week then?"

The Very First Day of Peace On Earth

Lance Corporal, Terence Blakely awoke to the sound of birdsong and distant folk music. He rolled out of bed and put on his slippers and dressing gown. He shuffled to the kitchen, switched on the kettle then went out to the front gate to get the morning paper. It was another sunny day. Peter Lacey, from two doors down, was at Terence's gate applying oil to its hinges.

"Good morning Pete!" said Terence.

"Hi Terry, I'm just going around to all the houses in the neighbourhood and oiling all the gates!"

"That's very thoughtful of you… thanks Pete!"

Across the road, Stan Lynch was helping Tony Hollier fix his fence. They both stopped work to bid Terence a good morning. A blossom scented breeze moved through the neighbourhood. A dozen teenagers were folk dancing on the Butterworth's front lawn. One of the dancers spotted Terence and ran over to him "Our music isn't too loud is it, Mister Blakely?"

"No Susie, its fine", he smiled "In fact it's quite pleasant!"

Terence picked up his newspaper and went back inside. He poured two cups of tea and looked at the paper. "WORLD PEACE AT LAST!" screamed the headlines. "NEW WORLD RELIGION SAVES THE WORLD! EVERY MOUTH ON THE PLANET FED!" There were no famous politicians anymore. They were all too busy helping each other to worry about their own egos. Terence carried the tea through to the bedroom and threw it over his wife's head.

Generations

The reason I nag you, young man, is because you don't listen to a goddamned word I say!

Cool it, Daddy-o, why're you so uptight?

Uptight? Bloody uptight? It's all right for you sitting around on your arse all day, smoking weed, living on handouts from responsible citizens like me. What about your future, lad? Where are you going to live, under a cardboard box? Who's going to pay your food bills?

Live in the *now*, Man, that's what this revolution is all about. Bread-heads like you are the reason why there's so many bad vibes in the world. You just run around all day in the rat race trying to own everything, so you can exploit the poor. Then for your recreation, you hang out with all the square phoneys and snort cocaine. That's not living, man. You're nothing but a *robot*! When was the last time you smelt a flower? When was the last time you watched a sunset? When was the last time you made love under a tree?

Oh phooey! When was the last time you had a bath? When was the last time you got off your arse and earned money from the fruits of your own labour? You're just stuck in some old mumbo-jumbo Sixties philosophy, like a scratched LP.!

What do you mean *old* Sixties philosophy? It *is* the Sixties, Daddy-o!

I'm sorry to tell you this, Sonny, but the year is 1989! Somewhere along the line, you've lost twenty years, dope-head!

Wait a minute, Daddy-o, what year were you born?

I was born on the 13th of October, 1951 — why?

But that's *my* birthday, man! Did you have a twin brother? — 'cos I know I didn't.

No, I didn't.

Woooh, heavy shit, man! So I'm, like, just talking to me, like?

Bloody hell, then what year is it now, then?

I don't know, man, but all this arguing can't be good for us —

I mean, ME.

Yeah, I agree, I'm going to cut down on my stress levels and stop snorting altogether.

Yeah, man, I'll meet you halfway — I'll get myself more motivated and give up the weed.

Yeah, it's a deal. I'll shake on that!

Bolt-Ons

Coonawarra is the smallest town in the whole universe. So when Abbie came up from Melbourne to stay with her Granny at Christmas, there may as well have been two suns rising in the East.

I knew Abbie must have liked me when she said my smoke rings were better than Dean Curtis's. Dean could blow smoke rings from one end of the barn to the other. Mine were always piss poor. It must be said that Abbie and Dean hated each other's guts. Dean said Abbie was a bitch and Abbie said Dean was immature. Abbie started sitting on my knee so I could blow smoke directly into her mouth, then we'd both watch to see how much of it she could exhale. Every time we did it, her lips would get closer and closer to mine. I thought smoking was the best invention ever. Dean didn't hang out with us anymore.

It was strange sitting in her Granny's dilapidated little kitchen sipping tea from a matching bone china teacup and saucer. If you looked close, in flowery writing, were the words 'Arrochar Hotel'. Her Granny had been a waitress there for decades, so I suppose she deserved to have a touch of stolen poshness at home. I'd look at her face and wonder how she could ever have been fifteen years old then I'd look at Abbie and have the same difficulty trying to imagine her at seventy.

The only reason I ever went there was because I liked getting a dink on the back of Abbie's bike. Abbie was a good strong rider but she was always kind of lady like too. Rattling down through Ferntree Gully was choice! I'd sneak my hands half way around her waist and hold on for dear life. Then she'd rise up on the pedals and give it hammer and tong up the other side. There was a short cut across Patterson's Creek. I'd carry the bike across first, the water coming half way up my thigh. Then she'd hitch her dress up and I'd piggyback her across. The rocks weren't half slippery and I'd feel her soft hair tickling my neck and face. I'd keep hitching her up higher and higher so that her face was right next to mine and her whole body was draped over me. I'd stop midstream pretending I didn't know the rocks like the back of my hand. She'd squeal directions straight into my ear. I could have walked around there for days on end.

We liked to play the smoking game in the back corner of the churchyard under the willow tree. On a still day the smoke would define columns of sunlight up through the branches. Sometimes she would squeeze the pimples on my face. It was the closet I'd ever been to a girl. We often went around looking at all the tombstones, wondering what kind of lives everyone had lived. Old Des Wenlock was the last person to be buried there. I asked Abbie to guess what kind of bloke he was. She imagined Des to have been a foreign diplomat who followed a local girl to Coonawarra and then after finding that his love was unrequited threw himself into Patterson's Creek whilst intoxicated. Abbie was right with the 'intoxicated' bit, Des was always pissed. On his tombstone it said 'Rest In Peace' which should have been attributed to his long-suffering widow who he pulverised on a weekly basis. No one in town recognised her without the bruises on her face.

Abbie used to write poems and do little drawings in an exercise book. That's when I learnt about Pete, the "Bolt-On." A "Bolt-On" is a rubberneck who bolts his surfboard onto his roof rack and never takes it off so he can look like a real surfer. Abbie had written all these crappy poems about him. When I told her I could draw good tattoos she let me draw a heart with a scroll on her arm but then I had to write 'Pete' in the scroll. That fucking hurt.

After a week she lost interest in the smoking game and though my smoke rings were improving she said she could hardly see them. She said that Bolt-On Pete was coming to pick her up on Saturday to take her down to Ninety-Mile Beach for the day. I got my own exercise book and worked frantically filling it with love poems to a girl named Michaela who lived on the outskirts of Lake Tyers. I told Abbie about all the great times Michaela and I had had together. How I'd thumb rides down to Lake Tyers every weekend with my surfboard. How we'd cling to one another as we got flushed through the canal and out into the surf at a hundred miles an hour, how we didn't care if we lived or died as long as we were together.

On the Friday I nicked my big sister's friendship ring and went and showed Abbie. I told her I was going to ask for Michaela's hand in marriage. It was the first time in two weeks that Abbie had shown any interest in anything I'd said or done. Abbie kept turning the ring in the sunlight, wearing it for five minutes then handing it back for five minutes. My heart sank every time she took it off.

On Saturday morning Dean and me waited behind the old water tank near the Tambo turnoff. When Pete and Abbie drove past we yelled out "Fucking Bolt On!" The tank gave us a choice echo. Then Dean yells out "Don't forget the water wings Bolt On!" Then I yelled out "Don't forget the skeg goes underneath else you'll cut your balls off!" Dean seemed to hate Bolt On Pete even more than me, he drew Pete on a ghost gum by the creek and blasted it with his dad's shotty. Dean and me were mates again.

Dean'd tell me about his sexual adventures with a sheila up north, called Claudia. Dean said that when Claudia orgasmed she yelled like a banshee and left claw marks in his back. I later found that exact same sentence in one of his porno books. He didn't even bother changing the name 'Claudia'. I told Dean how I had to fob Abbie away because she was getting jealous of Michaela. We both knew we were talking shit but untrue stories are better than nothin' in a town as crappy as Coonawarra.

Abbie's Granny died that following July and we never saw Abbie again. Dean and I would sometimes go look around the tombstones laughing at the phoney epitaphs and all the Bolt-On angels, trumpeting to Bolt-On heaven. Dean said the abo's were the only ones who weren't Bolt-Ons in Coonawarra. The day before school went back Dean and I gave each other love bites.

Very Late

I do *not* believe what I am seeing here! Candle light, everyone sitting in a circle holding hands like school children! It didn't take you long did it? I'm not even one hour late for this lodge meeting and you all decide to resort back to the old séance shenanigans that this society left behind decades ago! This certainly is an eye opener, Ladies and Gentlemen. All that time and effort we put into studying philosophy and science over the past six years, when all along you just wanted to play these preposterous games. Did you think I wasn't coming along tonight? When the cat's away, the mice will play! As it happened I was delayed in traffic – a three-car pile up near the Boundary Road turn off. Coming to think of it, it was a blessing in disguise: at least now I can see your true colours.

But Mister Malone, we set all this up for you!

Set it up for me? Have you taken leave of your senses Mrs Barnard? If I'd wanted entertainment, I would have gone along to the theatre or the circus tonight! My dear fellow Theosophists, please allow me to remind you all what the principal goal of the Theosophical Society is, as clearly stipulated back in 1896, and I quote: "To encourage studies in comparative religion, philosophy and science". Now, I'm afraid that what I'm seeing here before me tonight does not look like the investigation into any of those subjects in any shape or form.

But Mister Malone, please allow me to point out that it was also stipulated back in 1896 that another of Theosophy's goals was to investigate *the unexplained laws of nature and the powers latent in man*.

But Mrs Barnard, I don't think that includes lighting candles and holding hands whilst talking to people who are hiding under the table! That's old-hat, my dear! Even one of our principal founders, Madame Blavatsky was exposed more than once for employing side show techniques to create special effects during séances. Those séances were held simply as a means of attracting publicity to

Theosophy back then. Doctor Besant has long since disbanded all esoteric lodges worldwide. It's time that we all grew up and got back down to Theosophy's *real* work. Until any of you can present to me a single shred of *evidence* to support your preoccupation with spirits and life after death, this lodge will continue its studies in comparative religion, philosophy and science. Now will you all please stop holding hands: you have no idea how ridiculous you look!

But if we break the circle, Mister Malone, you'll disappear: you passed over to the other side a half an hour ago near the Boundary Road turn off. Mister Collins witnessed the whole thing and told us all as soon as he arrived.

Natural Selection

Two hundred different gangs of worshippers congregated outside the Pearly Gates. Between singing hymns and praying for the gates to open they elbowed, swore and spat at one another. Sometimes they even killed each other. In the hope of gaining spiritual one upmanship some gang leaders even tried to be friendly to one another but the Pearly Gates remained locked.

"Hey you!" shouted St. Peter. "You at the very back! Yes, you without the crucifix! What's your name?" The crowd fell silent.

"My name's Charles Darwin!" came the reply.

For the first time ever all the denominations became unified with hatred. "Crucify the heretic!" shouted one leader. "Knee cap him!" shouted another.

"Come forward, Mr Darwin!" commanded St. Peter.

Some worshippers tried to block his path, others, in search of brownie points, pushed the crowd back so that it parted like the Red Sea. Darwin, looking bewildered, slowly made his way up to the Gates.

"But surely you don't want *me* in there do you? I don't even believe in all this stuff," pleaded Darwin.

"Charles, you are surrounded by BELIEF. The Protestants and Catholics kill one another for their beliefs. Christianity has steadily evolved into over 200 different tribes of belief. They all have forgotten that mankind is a single species. It's God eat God out there, Charles, and each tribe wants to be king of the jungle – "DUCK!"

A Molotov cocktail sailed past Darwin's left ear. "God choosing you, Charles, just boiled down to *natural selection*!"

The Pearly Gates swung open and a monkey's paw the size of King Kong's reached out, picked up Darwin and carefully carried him inside.

The Tide Turns

Here, Daddy, let me rest the photo album on your legs so we can have a look at all the old family photographs together. Maybe that way you can get to know me a bit more. We've so much to catch up on, haven't we? Here help yourself to some crisps: they're salt and vinegar, your favourite.

Please Amanda, may I have a glass of water?

Daughter? Yes Daddy – I *am* your daughter – That's right – you *do* remember me don't you? *Now*, let's have a look at what we've got in here shall we? Ooh – look – here's an old black and white one – Mummy has written "January 1958" under it.

A drink, Mandy – I must have a drink.

That was the day I split my head open at the ice rink – I was in hospital for three weeks after that. It's a bit out of focus – Mummy took the photo – Do you remember where you were Daddy? You were at sea weren't you? Always at sea! And even when you *did* come home, you were always building those silly little model ships, weren't you? Mummy used to always say 'You can take the sailor out of the sea, but you can't take the sea out of the sailor'. Do you remember the time you beat Mummy up when one of the little masts got broken, do you remember that Daddy?

Water, a glass of water!

Daughter? Yes Daddy I *am* your daughter you *do* remember me don't you? Here Daddy have some salt and vinegar crisps, they're your favourite. I remembered your favourite, didn't I? Oh Daddy, here's a photo of me and Ronnie Housten swimming at Cornwall. It's a shame our heads are cut off. I think Mummy had had a few too many shandies when she took it! I remember she used to point at the ships in the distance and say that you were on one of them. I used to get so excited, but they never came any closer to the shore. Oh, we had such a laugh that weekend: poor mummy had to do weeks and weeks of overtime at the cafe to pay for that holiday; you always forgot to send us money, didn't you Daddy?

Water please?

Water? Oh Daddy, I'm so sorry. You've waited and waited and waited and waited for three days now and I completely forgot about you didn't I? My memory is like a sieve these days. Bad memories must run in the Wilson family, mustn't they Daddy? You forgot you had a little daughter to look after, didn't you? Even after Mummy died and you left the Merchant Navy – when I was stuck in that horrible children's home. The home kept writing to you, but you kept on forgetting and forgetting and forgetting and forgetting to make any contact.

Water!

Yes, us Wilsons certainly do have bad memories don't we Daddy? Mind you, years ago at school, I used to recite the first fifty elements on the periodical chart. But you wouldn't remember how clever I was, would you Daddy? It was Mummy who always helped me with my homework.

Water – Water!

Water? Water is H_2O – hydrogen hydroxide – two atoms of hydrogen to every one atom of oxygen, how's that? My memory is not as bad as I thought! Ooh look, here's a photo of me at the children's home at the Xmas party – that must have been about two months after Mummy threw herself off the Eastbourne Pier. That was my favourite dress. I remember that day very well: I'd spent all day getting ready because Mrs Humphries told me you were coming to take me out for the day to see Cinderella. Well, I waited and I waited and then at ten past nine, Mrs Humphries told me to put my pyjamas on and get ready for bed. She told me not to worry. She said you'd probably just forgotten. That's when the bed-wetting started. You forgot to telephone as well – yes – I *do* remember *that* day. I later found out that you were fishing with your old shipmates at Eastbourne. As Mummy used to always say "you can take the sailor out of the sea, but you can't take the sea out of the sailor!" To tell the truth Daddy, that's why I drugged you yesterday and shaved your beard off. It's because it always made you look like a sailor and it's time now to forget about the sea and remember me, your daughter! All your little model ships are now sailing across the English Channel, I gave them *all* to the ocean yesterday. Here, Daddy: have some crisps. They're salt and vinegar – your favourite. I didn't forget your favourite did I? And I didn't forget you, stuck in that old people's home neither, did I? I couldn't have that: my own flesh and blood stuck in there when I've got a lovely spare room here in my flat.

Amanda, please just wheel me over to the sink so I can get a drink myself.

I think it was the little outboard fishing boat you bought that pushed Mummy over the edge, when you painted "Veronica" on the bow and she found out that it was the name of one of your girlfriends, who you'd been sending your wages to.

For God's sake – you're killing me – I must have some water.

Daughter? Yes Daddy I *am* your daughter. Do you remember what Mummy used to say? "You can take the sailor out of the sea, but you can't take the sea out of the sailor!" But I think we're getting there, Daddy. It's like an exorcism. I can feel the tide slowly going out. Here, have some crisps – they're your favourite – salt and vinegar. Oh look! Here's an old black and white one of me in flares!

Players

Gwen Hobson had always considered herself to be a good Bingo player. But little did she realise that that single £100 Jackpot would be just the beginning of a string of Wednesday night Jackpots that would place her name indelibly into the history books of the great game. Week after week, she'd win the big one. The strange thing was that she never won any of the smaller draws. Gwen's best friend, Lorna O'Malley, put this phenomenon down to Gwen saving everything for the big finish.

Needless to say, there was a lot of suspicion brewing in the other corners of the hall, especially since some of the other players played with six books and Gwen only ever played with one. When interviewed by the local newspaper, she explained that she always got in a dither with more than one book.

Mavis Hickle, a six book player (who ousted Gwen from playing the church organ every Sunday, after notating all the bum notes Gwen played and handing her findings onto Father Kelso), began to get mighty suspicious after Gwen's fifteenth successive win. Mavis and her son, who was in charge of security at the Bingo Hall would pore over every frame of CCTV footage of Gwen arriving and leaving the venue (usually Gwen was carried upon her friends' shoulders to the bus stop), but they could find nothing untoward. They even tried switching the tables and chairs around beforehand, but Gwen just won on and on.

One morning, a Hello Magazine reporter and photographer arrived on Gwen's doorstep and, as Gwen had no other interests or hobbies to speak of, the reporter insisted on Gwen sitting behind the church organ for a photo shoot. Father Kelso explained to the reporter that Gwen had played at the church for the past twenty-two years and had only recently stepped down onto the substitution pew, so as to retain her energies for Wednesday evenings. But he had recently been informed from a higher source that her organ playing could in fact form part of her mid week Bingo preparations.

From that day forward, the church attendance soared, everyone wanted to hear Gwen's original interpretations of those boring old hymns. Only half a dozen green faces would shine out from the entranced congregation and those faces were seated upon the cold, hard sub's pew. And no other face was greener than that of Mavis Hickle. She would wince and tutt at every one of Gwen's improvisations.

"If only she'd break a finger or get the flu," thought Mavis, "then I could show the world what true musicianship was all about!"

But Gwen would have played that organ in an iron lung, if she had to – such was her ecstasy.

Almost on a par with her music comeback was the Wednesday night, when Queen Elizabeth II paid a visit. The Queen sat whispering at Gwen's table for over half an hour and then Gwen took the Queen around the hall, introducing her to some of the other players who were either squirming in their seats or running back and forth to the toilets. After Gwen had introduced the Queen to Mavis' table, Mavis whispered to her cronies that Gwen was just trying to rub their noses in it. But Gwen knew very well that, if she hadn't introduced Mavis to Liz (that's what Gwen and Gwen alone was allowed to call her), then she would never had heard the end of it.

Gwen Hobson was the natural choice to represent Great Britain in the World Bingo Championships that year in Mexico City. The greatest players from around the world all assembled under the one roof to battle it out, to find the world's greatest. A live coverage was shown on a giant television screen at the Brighton Town Hall, which was packed to capacity. Gwen got off to a tremendous start, seemingly putting pen to paper at the announcement of every number. But, as she looked down on that little blue book of numbers, strange things started happening to her mind. She could see venomous eyes looking out at her through all the zeros. She could hear whispers from Mavis Hickle's table spiralling around and around in her head. Numbers – organ notes – whispers – cameras flashing. She blocked her ears and closed her eyes.

BEEENGO!

A rotund Mexican woman was gibbering and jumping up and down, kissing a crucifix that hung from her neck. Then, a dozen scruffy children ran to her from the sidelines, along with the cameramen and reporters. Tears streamed down Gwen's face in relief and joy at the loving sight that befell her.

Gwen's best friend, Lorna O'Malley, ran over to her and told her not to cry – she should be proud of having made it to the world championships. Then Lorna looked over Gwen's numbers and found that she should have been the winner, had she bothered to mark the last number off. Gwen told Lorna not to tell anyone, as she'd be the laughing stock of Brighton. Officially, Gwen put her defeat down to the Hello! Magazine Curse. Gwen never won another Jackpot and the church congregation dwindled back to normal. Mavis Hickle replaced Gwen on the organ.

Jackpots didn't bother Gwen anymore. She just loved the Bingo atmosphere – she could carve it with a knife – that giddy dizziness, that passive smoking always bought to her, the free cups of tea and digestive biscuits. All those faces that she knew so well, the ones that would gaze at her in awe or shoot daggers at her. She was glad to be free of all that now. She was happy just taking part in that big game of life that is Bingo!

The Self Portrait

Nigel Smith had been an accountant for seventeen years. Enough said. But one day his boss assigned him to audit at the Tate Modern. The manager of the gallery even invited Nigel along to an important exhibition. Normally he wouldn't have bothered attending but he calculated that if he consumed nine glasses of wine and a belly full of free food, he would save himself twenty-seven pounds and forty two pence.

There were a lot of very weird people at the gallery. One exhibit consisted of a human foot sewn onto the neck of a stuffed dog; another piece was a car tyre dipped in wax, but Nigel took it all in his stride. The wine was very good and there were lots of half-naked women to gawp at. When Nigel stubbed a cigarette out in the ashtray an important looking weirdo ran over and proclaimed the ashtray a masterpiece. Soon the whole gallery had gathered around "Oohing and "Aahing" at Nigel's creation. Nigel Smith had clearly stolen the show. The ashtray was immediately submitted for the Albanto Prize in Paris.

Nigel flew out to Paris but quickly tired of the art crowds fawning all over him. He drank too much wine at the award night and when he was announced as the winner, promptly threw up on the carpet. The carpet was carefully torn up from the floor, framed and submitted for the Kelly Modern Sculpture Award in New York.

Staggering drunk, off the plane in New York, he was greeted by the paparazzi. When asked how he went about creating his art he replied "The art is creating the artist and I have nothing to do with it, now will you all just fuck off and leave me alone!" After Nigel won the Kelly Modern Sculpture Award the television footage of his outburst was entered into the short film category at the Canne Film Festival but by this time Nigel Smith had had enough. He flew directly to London and tried to fit back into his old job, auditing at the Tate Modern. But things could never be the same.

On his first day back at work his dirty coffee cup went missing as did his waste paper basket and doodle pad. People even started to follow him to the toilet in the hope that he would leave a new sculpture behind. Nigel was the loneliest man in the world. That evening he made his way downstairs and hung himself in the main gallery. His choice of venue and perfect timing for this tragic performance clinched him the Turner Prize.

Paper Anniversary

"I think it's about time you decided who you're married to, Anthony: me or that newspaper!"

Anthony licked his thumb and turned another page "What's that, Tracey?"

"You don't even know what day it is, do you Anthony? Every night for the past twelve months, you've just come home from your office, plonked your arse on that couch and opened that bloody newspaper out in front of your face. All I ever see is your body with a front page looking back at me. You don't pay any attention to me anymore. That newspaper is nothing but a wall between us Anthony!"

Anthony placed the opened newspaper on the coffee table and removed his reading glasses. Crying had devastated Tracey's make-up. Streams of mascara inked her pretty face.

"That's not true, Baby! This newspaper is one of the best sources of communication in the whole country. The information in here concerns you and I directly, whether it's the price of food on the table or what the politicians are saying and don't forget, Tracey. If you hadn't been a page three girl, we would never have met in the first place! This newspaper built this house and it allows us to enjoy the lifestyle we enjoy."

"We enjoy? We enjoy? Anthony, I've just become a trophy of yours that you show off to your snotty friends like all your other possessions. You're fifty seven, you're slowing down but I'm only twenty-two years old and I'm lonely and bored Anthony. Don't you understand that?"

"Tracey – Honey, come back, what are you doing?"

"You'll see, if you can keep your head out of that newspaper for two minutes!"

Tracey stormed back into the living room and stood by the open fire.

"Tracey what are you doing? That's our wedding album!"

"I'm going to throw it in the fire!"

"Honey NO! That's our memories in there – we can't replace those photos!"

"OK, then, Anthony – come over here now and throw that newspaper in the fire – *now Anthony!*"

"But I haven't read the – "

"*Now*, Anthony, else I'll throw this album in. It's us or that newspaper, it's *your* decision!"

As it happened, the newspaper and the photo album were thrown in simultaneously. Anthony tried to retrieve the album, but Tracy managed to drag his heavy frame away. Anthony bellowed and lunged towards the fire. He tripped on the rug and landed head long amongst the flames. Sparks and cinders flew about the room as he rolled across the floor clutching his chest.

"My pills Tracy – get my pills!"

Tracey grabbed a bottle of Valium from the bedroom but she didn't return to her husband. Instinctively, she drove to the seaside resort where they'd spent their honeymoon, stopping for a bottle of their favourite whiskey on the way.

Tracey awoke to the familiar sound of a newspaper being flagged open. Anthony smiled at her from the bench opposite her. But this Anthony was in his early twenties – handsome and smiling at her warmly – his unmoving face was grafted onto the front page of a newspaper held before the old newspaper reading Anthony. Above the smiling Anthony's face were the headlines NEWSPAPER MAGNATE DEATH RIDDLE.

"Anthony? Is that you? Help me darling, I can't move"

The newspaper lowered to reveal a bespectacled face she'd never seen before. The empty whiskey bottle smashed as she raced from the waiting room. The whole railway station spun around her as she found her way to the toilet, there, she gulped down the last of her pills then carefully made her way outside.

She awoke in the middle of the night to see a figure placing newspapers over her shivering body.

"You'll be surprised how warm these'll keep you, Pet!"

Tracey thought the vagrant was Anthony and drifted off into a deep sleep, feeling more loved than she ever had in their three hundred and sixty-five days of marriage.

Twister

"Dorothy, please don't come into my Emerald Castle with all that 'Over The Rainbow' tosh!"

"But, Great Wizard of Oz, that's where my home is – over the rainbow – in Kansas! *There's no place like home*."

"But Dorothy, Dear, there's more than one rainbow in the sky, isn't there?"

"W-what do you mean, Great Wizard?"

"That other rainbow that runs directly from Kansas to down town Hollywood, that's what I mean JUDY!"

"P-pardon me?"

"Your *real* name is Judy Garland not Dorothy, so don't come skipping in here with that mutt and those other three hangers' on, pining about your home back in Kansas where you've probably never even been before. So let us take a look at that *other* rainbow, Judy. The one that runs from Kansas over to your home or should I just say *house*!"

"OK, Great Wizard."

"It's a lovely big house, isn't it, Judy? But do you really feel *at home* there? Speak up Judy!"

"N-no!"

"So, if you don't feel at home in your *very own* house, tell me Judy, tell the *whole world* Judy." Where *do* you feel at home?"

"O-on the stage o-or in the s-studio."

"Ah! Now we're getting somewhere Judy, don't you see? That rainbow has come full circle hasn't it? It goes from here back to Kansas and from Kansas over to your house in Hollywood and from there over to here: your real home – *here and now* in the studio! So, *home* isn't over some silly old 'pie in the sky' rainbow, is it? Stop chasing rainbows, girl! Kick off those red shoes and skip out that door marked 'Exit', turn left and follow that black bitumen road, through those big gates out into the real world, Judy. Forget rainbows, forget contracts , forget pep pills! It's up to you, girl, now go!"

This whole scene was left on the cutting room floor. Judy Garland couldn't ever leave the stage or studio for long and lived happily never after.

Anarchy In The U.S.A.

A forty one year old punk in full seventy's regalia scaled the front wall to the L.A. Mansion. He raced across the manicured lawn towards the house, but was immediately accosted by three deafening Dobermans. The mohawked warrior fended off the sleek beasts as best as he could with his union jack painted Doc Martens and was about to be mauled, when a lordly figure emerged at the front entrance to the mansion.

"Heel boys! Sit now – sit!"

With robotic obedience, the three beasts dropped their backsides to the green.

"What business do you have here on my property, then?" called the Lord of the Manor.

"It's me, John – Wilbur Anderson – we used to squat together back in seventy-six in South London – before you hit the big time with the Sex Pistols!"

The dressing gowned Johnnie Rotten made his way down the marbled steps and strode across the lawn to the weedy punk. He tossed a biscuit to each dog and commanded them back to their quarters.

"Well fuck me, Wilbur, the last time I saw you was on the T.V. kickin' the front window out of McDonalds at that Poll Tax March! How the fuck did you afford to get over this side of the planet then?"

"Let's just say, Johnnie, that a kindly old lady handed me two grand and an L.A. street map and tossed me on a plane - but more about me later! I want to know what happened to *you*, John. Just look at yourself: an L.A. mansion; a Mercedes Benz; Mister respectable payin' your taxes; no drugs – you're a fucking disgrace!"

"Fuck Wilbur, I earned all this, you know that! I worked hard for these rewards!"

"That's bollocks John, and you know it! You made one fuckin' record then cashed in as the King of anarchy – you fucking hypocrite!"

Wilbur rolled up his tattered sleeve and pointed to an anarchy symbol tattooed on his arm.

"Have you forgotten what *values* are, John? You should change your name to John Filthy – *filthy fucking rich*! Anarchy put you where you are today and look at yourself: your whole life's in fucking perfect order! I bet your sprogs go to college in Limos!

"All right Wilbur, if you've just come here to slag me, you can piss off right now!"

"I bet you have Maggie Thatcher round for tea and caviar sandwiches, you fucking yuppie!

"Right Wilbur – That's it! – *Off* my property now else I'm calling the police!"

"Just listen to yourself John – *you're one of them for fuck's sake*! And guess what Mister *Filthy*: we've got this whole place surrounded. All your old buddies from your squatting days have migrated and, just for old time's sake, we've cut all the electricity off! Your puppy dogs are scoffing jelly laced burgers right this minute!"

"All right Wilbur, if you're all such Anarchy Purists, how the fuck did you all afford the air fares over here?"

"Well Johnnie, as I said before, a kindly old lady gave us each two grand and your address and told us we could squat here for ever and ever – *God save the Queen. I mean it man!* Ha! Ha!"

"You mean the *Queen* paid all your fucking fares over here to *squat* on *my* property?"

"Yeah, it's part of all that Golden Jubilee Celebrations stuff – mind you it *was* all Prince Harry's brain wave!"

"Prince Harry hey? I should have known he'd pull something like this – that dope smoking little PUNK!"

The Invasion

A father and son sit on a beach beneath a starry sky.

"Do you think there is life out there, Dad?"

"I'd like to think so son, but we'll probably never know."

"But Dad, what about the stories going around about beings from another world having already been here and taken animals and plant samples back with them?"

"Ha! Ha! Don't believe everything that Uncle of yours tells you!"

"But Dad, he said these beings look like ghosts and they're going to return in greater numbers and take over with weapons that could wipe us all out in a flash – they killed seven before they left."

"Oh calm down son – I'll believe it all when I see it!"

"But its true Dad. They've gone back to their world – its called England - and they'll be coming back here in canoes as high as gum trees filled with countless ghost people."

"Come on son, get your boomerang and spears, we have a long walk back to camp and I'm going to have a word with your Uncle Abor when we get there!"

Two hundred and twenty-six years later another father and son sit on that same beach. The son looks up at the starry sky and asks: "Do you think there's life out there, Dad?"

Goddesses

The Chambermaid entered the Palatial Suite at 11.32 a.m. Whilst vacuuming under the dressing table, she caught sight of herself in the mirror and was shocked at what she saw: she looked so much older than her 32 years. In an attempt to cheer herself up, she tried on the Movie Legend's evening gown, then she carefully applied some make-up, complete with a beauty spot on her left cheek, then to finish the job off, she donned the platinum blonde wig and added a generous spray of Chanel No.5. She sat on the bed and broke into tears. All she'd ever wanted was to be a Movie Star, and now that she was three months pregnant, she'd have to marry a taxi driver. Her time had well and truly ran out.

    The real Movie Star entered the Palatial Suite at 11.32 p.m. She tore off the platinum blonde wig and threw it on the floor, then wiped off her make-up with her hands. She ripped off her evening gown in disgust . Whilst vacuuming a line of cocaine up through a rolled hundred dollar bill, she caught sight of herself in the mirror. She was shocked at what she saw and, with another three films lined up, time had well and truly run out. She sat on the bed and broke into tears. All she'd ever wanted to be was a housewife.

Speed Dating

She told me *her* ex was emotionally constipated and had never showed his true feelings.

I told her *my* ex read Betty Shine books and was away with the fairies.

She told me *her* ex was a miser who gave her a ten pound weekly allowance.

I told her *my* ex had played around behind my back and scarred me for life.

She told me *her* ex broke her nose in a drunken rage.

I told her *my* ex suffered PMT and nearly scratched my eye out.

She told me *her* ex chose what clothes she could wear before leaving the house.

I told her *my* ex vacuumed twice a day just so I couldn't hear the football.

She told me *her* ex had completely shattered her confidence and that she'd been alone for two years and four months.

At that point I took my bifocals from my top pocket and put them on and she drew the hair away from eyes and looked up at me. We *were* each other's ex's.

It was then that we decided to give things another try.

The Great Escape

Just as I drove around a tight bend on the rainforest highway – there she was – hitching by the side of the road wearing a mother of pearl necklace. I pulled up beside her and I asked her where she was heading. "As far as you can take me into the rainforest" she answered "So where are you heading?" "As far away form the office as I can get! – Jump in"

She sat cross-legged in the passenger seat. She had a big bush of auburn hair with strands of coloured cotton and beads woven in here and there. "So you've escaped from your office have you?"

"Yeah, I just up and left at seventeen minutes to twelve this morning." The car wove its way through dappled shadows. "Before I left my office, I typed on my computer screen 'fuck computers, fuck nine to five, fuck the city, fuck junk food, fuck traffic jams, fuck pretend happiness, fuck the mortgage, fuck the pension, fuck caffeine and anti-depressants, fuck Morley and Rothschild Ltd, fuck *everything* I quit!' Then I spun around on my swivel chair, stood up, marched to the lift, went down to the ground floor got in my car and drove away – and *here* I am."

She sat there gawping at me then she said "And here *I* am. Do you think you'll ever go back?"

"I'd rather *die* than turn back now. I'm forty-six years old and I've done nothing with my life. My life's a big charade. I want to grow dreadlocks, take my shoes and socks off, wear a sarong, swim naked in a river, watch the sun come up, grow my own pineapples and slash the tops off with a machete, and let the juice run onto my tongue."

She was rolling a fat joint. "Wow, it must be scary for a guy your age to make a break away from everything like this. What's your name anyway?"

"Winston"

"My name's Liberty. I think you're fucking cool doing what you're doing, Winston. You might be just one man escaping the rat race, but thousands will follow you when they see that it can be done!"

"Wow," I said. "I've never been called 'cool' before."

"There's just *one* thing, Winston. You'll have to let me take that neck tie off you."

She threw it straight out the window. I saw it hit the road in the rear vision mirror, then it disappeared into the dust like an angry snake.

"Yeah, that *does* feel better. I can really breathe now!"

"Breathe in all that fresh air Winston and here, take a toke on this it was grown right here in the rainforest." I took a long draw and here eyes and the mother of pearl necklace were one. She placed her hand on my shoulder "You're living right on the edge Winston – typing up stories during working hours. You could get a verbal warning for that!"

I spun around in my swivel chair. It was Liberty wearing her mother-of-pearl necklace. She started reading what I'd typed on the screen:

The Great Escape. Just as I drove around a tight bend on the rainforest highway – there she was – hitching by the side of the road.

I darkened the screen. "You're taking a big gamble Winston I never realised you were so brave!" I imagined her hair brushed out with pieces of coloured cotton and beads woven into it. "Mr. Morley sent me down to say that you are not to leave the office till the McCloud Account is finished."

"Tell Mr Morley I'll stay on all night if I have to". "Here let me straighten that tie Winston, it's all over the place! I'm free this weekend we could go for a picnic in Koala Forest if you want."

"I've got the Gaynor Accounts and the Portman project to do yet. I'll be tied up all weekend and possibly the next."

Liberty rolled her eyes "Mr. Morley is buying pizza for everyone as there won't be time for lunch breaks. Do you want the usual?"

"Yeah, an Hawaiian with a large pineapple juice thanks – freshly squeezed if possible."

Bestiality

Graham unleashed the Labrador who ran directly over to a French poodle who was running freely around the park.

"Fido! Come here, now!" yelled Graham but he didn't mean it because the poodle belonged to Thelma McGuiness. Thelma had been the apple of Graham's eye for the past five and a half years. Thelma arose from the park bench and trilled "Peaches! Come here this minute!" but she didn't mean it either because she too had the hots for Graham.

"That dog doesn't listen to a word I say!" muttered Graham, "I've got him for a week while my brother's away." Thelma gave him an understanding smile. Had Graham known of the social opportunities dog walking would open to him, he would have gotten a dog of his own years ago. "Come away from that muddy ground!" yelled Thelma. She turned to Graham. "It's a losing battle, having a white dog in weather like this!" The dogs danced around each other, licking noses and snapping excitedly. Fido was entranced with Peaches' neatly trimmed coat. "Yes," said Graham, "they say it's the third wettest March we've had in the past fifteen years." Thelma sat back down on the bench. "I can believe that: it's rained every single day this week. Do you think it's got something to do with that global warming thing?"

Graham rubbed his left leg. "Ooh, that knee's playing up again", his knee was fine. He sat down beside Thelma, gazed into the distance and began a discourse on the three levels of the ozone, warm fronts, cold fronts and isobars. Thelma noticed a tuft of hair peeking out from his open-neck shirt. This was the closest they'd ever been together. Her gaze wandered up and down his face then rested on his inviting lips. Behind the park bench, Fido and Peaches were in the throes of passion. Peaches' head swung from left to right, licking Fido's dangling tongue.

When Graham's weather monologue came to a close,

Thelma responded with her recent observations on the high and low pressure systems in the area, as well as the acid rain and wind chill factors. Graham was hypnotised by Thelma's dangling earring that swung from her beautiful earlobe. When Thelma's monologue petered out, there was an embarrassing silence. Then, Thelma said "My name's Thelma, by the way!" Graham knew very well what her name was. He replied "Thelma? That's a nice name. I had a great Aunt called Thelma. My name's Graham. I live just around the corner in Short Avenue. I'm sure I've seen you around the neighbourhood once or twice before." Four hundred and fifty times would have been more accurate. Every time Thelma had walked past Graham's house, he had raced to the window, drooling.

"I live in Short Avenue too" said Thelma. "I'm at number seventeen." "Oh!" said Graham. "I'm at eleven. That's just a few doors away." "It's a small world" said Thelma, and they shared a nervous laugh.

Behind the bench, Fido and Peaches were scaling the zenith of canine ecstasy. Peaches groaned softly in Fido's firm embrace.

"I – I was wondering Thelma, if – if you weren't doing anything tomorrow afternoon, if you'd like to pop over for a cup of tea or – or coffee or a herb tea, if you'd prefer?" Fido lay gasping amongst some daffodils in euphoric exhaustion. Peaches licked his rubberised face, in appreciation. "I'd really like to come over, Graham, but I'm flying out to Australia tomorrow morning. Peaches and I are going to live with my sister in Sydney – she's my only family and I was getting to feel quite lonely here." "Oh well" shrugged Graham, trying to look unaffected. "It's no big deal – just a spur of the moment thing. Well, I hope you enjoy yourself down under: plenty of sunshine and not so much mud to worry about!"

Graham glanced around to see the dogs well into their

second round of lovemaking. He screamed "Fido! Come here now!" This time, he meant every word, but Fido had his priorities sorted and continued giving Peaches everything he was worth. Graham strode over and attached the chain to Fido's collar and, with an almighty jerk, ripped him away from Peaches. He bid farewell to Thelma and viciously tugged Fido along the path. When they disappeared from view into Short Avenue, Thelma heard a short sharp yelp.

Too Big For My Boots

It was an argument I'd heard a thousand times before. The teaspoon was getting the tea all stirred up, saying that if it weren't for him, the tea would be unpalatable. The tea spouted that the whole tea room revolved around her and that everything else was of secondary importance. The tea cup chipped in "But, what about me? The tea would run straight through the floor boards without a cup to sit in." Then the saucer clattered "Tea cups are frowned upon without saucers, here, supporting you, keeping you in place and catching your spillage!" The tablecloth said "But look who's here beneath everyone on the whole table? If I were snatched away right now, you'd all be doomed!"

"But what about me?" said I. "You'd all be just inanimate objects, if it wasn't for my fragmented personality!" This got everyone on the table shaking and clattering. I drew the four corners of the tablecloth together and they all tumbled about like fish caught in a net. I swung them around my head then launched them at the tea room window. They all let out a deafening final scream. "Every single one of your lives rested solely upon me!" I cried. "And you should never have forgotten that!" "Speaking of solely," said my shoes in unison, "… you're resting solely upon us this very second." "My life doesn't rest solely upon you two!" I yelled, whilst forcing them to stamp on each other. "I can easily replace you both with a new pair of shoes." "Yes," said the left one. "But don't forget, we're not the only shoes with tongues!" They laughed together, as they marched me out of the café and stood me in the path of an oncoming bus.

The Electric Hare & The Silicone Bunny

It is the night before the biggest Greyhound Racing Event of the year – The Gabriel Cup. Mark Wood is fast asleep dreaming of his dog 'Zorro' winning the big race by ten lengths. He sees himself being presented with the big gold cup by the 2003 Layboy Bunny of the Year, Norma Silicona. The champagne flows and Mark accepts an invitation back to Norma's penthouse.

Meanwhile, back in the real world in Mark's backyard, Zorro is fast asleep in the midst of a glorious doggie dream. The race starts and he sees himself shoot ahead of the pack. The world flies past as he draws ever nearer to the bobbing cottontail. The hare's enticing scent of fear slipstreams into his nostrils as it comes into reach. Never before had he gotten so close to the damned thing!

Meanwhile, back in Mark's dream, he is burying his face between Norma's double G breasts. They have sex fifteen times over the next three hours and between each session Norma fetches Mark c old beers from the fridge and cooks him huge servings of chicken Vindaloo and tells him what a great dog trainer and lover he is.

Meanwhile, back in Zorro's dream, Zorro sinks his salivating jaws into the hare's soft neck and lifts it off the rail. It is an exquisite specimen, the biggest he has ever seen, but beautifully proportioned. He shakes the prey vigorously side to side till the kicking and squealing stop. The taste of fresh blood oozes into his mouth. When the rest of the pack arrive, they all know better than to touch his trophy. They can only look on and drool.

Meanwhile, back in Mark's dream, all of his punting friends have arrived at the penthouse. The conversation centres on Mark's great achievements and Tubby Sinclair admits that the only reason he beat Mark in the Brickmaker Arms Pool Tournament was because of the roll in the table. Nobody dares to make a move on Norma – they can only gaze at her cleavage and drool though, she is kind enough to autograph posters for everyone.

Meanwhile, back in Zorro's dream, the one that always got away is now slowly filling his skinny guts. As a consolation prize to the others he leaves a few succulent scraps for the others to fight over. He takes a nap in a daisy filled meadow with a few admiring bitches, whilst the race organisers frantically try to find an equally superb hare to replace the eaten one. He snoozes away, happy in the knowledge that the most exclusive unobtainable cuisine is now his for the taking whenever he so chooses to take it.

Back in the real world, the two dreamers awake early and go to the big race. Zorro doesn't catch the big hare and finishes ninth over the line. Later on in the evening, Mark has his face slapped by Trish Norris, who later goes home with Tubby Sinclaire. But Mark and Zorro still have their dreams in their hearts to get them up out of bed at 5.00 a.m. the next morning to train and strive on towards those ultimate goals of triumph – The Electric Hare and the Silicone Bunny.

Reality T.V.

The Ruben family loved reality T.V. and the realer it got, the more they loved it. Who needs Eastenders, Coronation Street, Neighbours or Home and Away when you can see the real thing? They loved real interaction, real passion, real arguments, and real love.

Sure, the storylines took longer to develop and weren't as spectacular as the soaps, but the Ruben family felt that it was well worth the wait.

One night, Mister Ruben went to turn the television on and something popped inside the set. All eyes followed a tiny wisp of smoke to the ceiling, then the family gazed in disbelief into their own long reflections in the vacant screen.